MY LIFE OF CRIME
The collected memoirs of
Detective Inspector Peter Johns

JUDY FORD

MY LIFE OF CRIME.

Published by Bernie Fazakerley Publications

This book is a work of fiction. Any references to real people, events, establishments, organisations or locales are intended only to provide sense of authenticity and are used fictitiously. All of the characters and events are entirely invented by the author. Any resemblances to persons living or dead are purely coincidental.

No part of this book may be used, transmitted, stored or reproduced in any manner whatsoever without the author's written permission.

ISBN: 1-911083-20-1
ISBN-13: 978-1-911083-20-7

CONTENTS

INTRODUCTION

These short stories have previously been published as individual e-books. They also appear on the website https://sites.google.com/site/llanwrdafamily/, as entries in DI Peter Johns' memoirs.

Peter Johns grew up in a children's home. On leaving school, he entered the police force. A chance encounter led to his transfer to CID, after which he began slow but steady progress up the promotion ladder to Detective Inspector.

Reaching the heights of Detective Sergeant gave him the courage to propose to the love of his life, Jamaican nurse Angie Wheeler. Their long and happy marriage was blessed with two children: Hannah, who followed her mother into nursing, and Edward, who chose a career in computers.

Tragedy struck shortly before their silver wedding anniversary when Angie was knifed and killed in a racially-motivated attack – an event from which Peter never fully recovered.

Three years later, he married his friend of more than twenty years, Bernie Fazakerley, and moved in with her and her young daughter, Lucy. His new family was later augmented by the arrival of DCI Jonah Porter, a disabled colleague and long-standing family friend.

These memoirs are Peter's attempt to make sense of his eventful life and unconventional family.

PC JOHNS TURNS TO CRIME

(I make the transition from Bobby on the beat to
Criminal Investigation Department)

1 Bobby on the Beat

When I left school, I had to find some sort of job right away, because, having been brought up in a children's home, I didn't have the option of staying with Mum and Dad until I could make up my mind what to do with my life. The police appealed to me because I thought it was a job where I could feel that I was making a difference – keeping people safe, that sort of thing. I suppose it probably also provided me with the security of a big institution – a bit like the one I was leaving – and somewhere to live.

So I applied to join Thames Valley Police and was accepted on their training course. I spent three years as a beat officer in East Oxford, which I enjoyed very much; but while I was there, I got dragged into the investigation of a murder case and that made me start to think that what I really wanted was to join CID. That was also the case that brought me into contact with my future boss, Richard Paige, for the first time, which probably also had something to do with my change of direction.

I've told you about my having been brought up in care, not to make you feel sorry for me, but because it has a bearing on this case. I'm eternally grateful for the great start in life that the National Children's Home gave me, and I don't feel that I missed out at all by not knowing my birth parents. But one thing that being in a home did give me was more than average experience of the bad things that can go on inside a family and the difficulties that children – and their parents – sometimes face. I was luckier than a lot of the children that passed through the home that I lived in. My mother handed me over shortly after I was born and I stayed there until I left school. Some kids were in and out of care like yo-yos or came to the home after years of misery with parents who were inadequate or even downright cruel.

It was having that background that made me feel for a single mother – I'll call her Jenny – who lived on my patch with her five kids. I don't know where their father was – he was long gone before I knew the family. Indeed, it wouldn't surprise me if the boys all had different fathers. And it was having lived with kids from that sort of family that helped me, as a green PC, to get under the skin of the boy who turned out to have the key to the whole case, when my elders and betters were floundering.

2 MISSING PERSON

It didn't start as a murder. At first, we thought it was 'just' a missing child. Of course, for the parents, a missing child could never be less than terrifying, but we did assume at the beginning that there was a good chance that everything would turn out OK in the end.

I was involved from the start because it was a family that I'd got to know quite well through having several times had to escort one or more of its younger members home after they'd been found spraying graffiti on walls or sneaking magazines out of the corner shop without paying for them. There were five boys, ranging in age from seven upwards, with the oldest being fifteen. As I said before, their father had left home long ago and their mother was finding it hard to cope. She had to work long hours at various low-paid jobs in order to make ends meet. That meant that, for most of the day, Michael, the oldest, was left in charge of the younger ones.

These days they'd probably have ASBOs served on them and be given Community Service to keep them occupied, but this was back in nineteen seventy and things were different. Single mothers like Jenny were rather frowned upon by the middle-class matrons of more salubrious parts of Oxford, but, on the other hand, there was a certain amount of 'boys will be boys' attitude that allowed her youngsters to get away with more than might be the case these days. I found myself giving them repeated reprimands, but it never got to the stage where I thought of charging them or giving them a formal police caution.

Actually, they were quite nice boys underneath – full of high spirits and, above all, loyal to one another – which is more than can be said of a lot of brothers! Anyway, with that history behind them, we didn't take it very seriously when Ian, aged twelve, didn't arrive home from school one evening.

To be fair to the police, the family didn't report it until the following day. Michael told his mother, when she got home late in the evening, after a stint in the kitchens at one of the colleges. Then she dithered about telling anyone, because she was worried that Social Services might wade in and take the children away from her if she had to admit that she'd left a teenager in charge of four younger siblings. So by the time we got the call, any trail that there may have been was cold.

When Jenny finally got round to reporting that Ian was missing, she did it by calling in at the local police station. She was so hesitant and confused that at first the desk sergeant didn't take her seriously. Then, when she persisted – and perhaps more importantly when Michael started shouting at him to listen to her – he called me and sent me back home with them to talk with the whole family about what had happened.

Looking back, this was a totally inadequate response, but I suppose he thought they were trouble-makers and that it was all a storm in a teacup that would right itself soon enough.

When I got there, the two youngest boys were huddled up together on the sofa, looking scared out of their wits, and Paul, aged thirteen, who had been left in charge while Jenny and Michael went down to the station, was standing over them with his fists clenched. I wasn't sure whether this was to intimidate them or to ward off anyone who might try to attack the family.

I asked Jenny to make a cup of tea, to keep her busy while I talked to the boys. They were wary at first, but Michael told them to answer my questions and it wasn't long before they started to open up a bit.

I soon realised that things were serious. Paul, after a lot of coaxing, told me that Ian had been the subject of bullying ever since he moved up to secondary school – particularly on the way home. It had got so bad that he'd started bunking off before the last lesson of the day in order to get away before the bullies got out. He couldn't get into the house until Michael got home, so he would hang around on street corners until his brother returned.

What made the alarm bells start ringing for me was when Paul said that Ian had struck up a friendship with a man whom he had met on the streets. It all sounded very innocent on the face of it – just a matter of the man taking him into a café to get him out of the rain sometimes and giving him occasional packets of crisps and cans of pop – but it made me very uneasy. These days we'd talk about *grooming*, but, as I said, this was the nineteen seventies.

I told Jenny that I had no choice but to call in CID and organise a proper search for Ian. Michael made a lot of fuss about this idea – which was quite rich, seeing as he was the one who was so indignant that the police weren't taking them seriously. I suppose he was afraid that Ian – or the family as a whole – would be in trouble.

So there we were, with a full-scale hunt going on for young Ian, and Detective Inspector Paul Murdishaw in charge of what we all hoped would not turn out to be a murder enquiry. Murdishaw's assistant was a certain Detective Sergeant Richard Paige, a gentle giant with pale yellow hair and penetrating blue eyes. He didn't say much, but I could see that he was watching the family closely and taking everything in.

3 GATHERING EVIDENCE

I spent a lot of time with the family, being the point of contact between them and the team that were investigating the disappearance. As time went on and Ian still did not return home, we started to get more and more anxious that he might have been abducted or else had some sort of accident. House to house enquiries drew a blank, and there were very few responses to appeals in the local paper and on the radio for witnesses to come forward. I began to feel very helpless at having to go back to Jenny time and time again to tell her that we were no further forward.

Then I noticed that the youngest boy, Anthony, was looking particularly uncomfortable and kept starting to speak and then being interrupted by Paul. I tried to get him on his own to ask him what was bothering him, but it was a small house and he stayed very close to James, the second youngest, who was the only other one still at Primary School. In the end, I confided to Inspector Murdishaw my suspicions that Anthony might know more than he was letting on.

Murdishaw grilled the boys – for the third or fourth time – but they all insisted that they knew nothing at all about where Ian might have gone after school or who his mysterious friend might be. I began to think that I was imagining things and that I'd made a bit of a fool of myself with Murdishaw.

Sergeant Paige, however, thought differently. He realised that the boys were wary of authority and frightened of Murdishaw's rather hectoring manner. He collared me in the canteen one lunchtime and cross-examined me about the family and in particular the boys. I told him everything that I could think of about them, and I was surprised to realise just how much that was.

Michael saw himself very much as the man of the family and had several times been in trouble for using his fists rather too freely in defence of his younger brothers. He was a strapping lad, already nearly six foot tall and well-built. He had recently left school and was working as a labourer on a building site in Cowley. In his self-imposed role as bread-winner, he worked long hours in order to bring in as much cash as he could to supplement his mother's meagre wages.

I liked Michael – although he'd often crossed swords with me when I'd caught him or his brothers up to no good – and was of the opinion that he, rather than Jenny, was what kept the family together and out of serious trouble with the police.

His untidy mop of black hair, penetrating brown eyes and swarthy complexion put me in mind of an Italian brigand from the old-fashioned adventure stories that I remember one of my primary school teachers reading to us; and I suppose there was something Sicilian about his fierce family loyalty – like the mafia. His appearance, together with his rather aggressive approach to anyone who might pose a threat to his family – be they police, social services or local residents incensed at damage to their property – probably explains why he had a reputation in the neighbourhood as a tough guy and someone to steer clear of.

As I related all this to Paige, it dawned on me that, now that Michael was working full-time, there would be long periods when the other boys were unsupervised, presumably with Paul acting as minder for the younger ones. I was much less confident of Paul's ability to undertake that role. To my mind, he was the least likeable of the five boys, being always on the defensive and clearly resentful of Michael's power. I could well imagine that he might have over-stepped the mark in imposing his own authority on them. He was small and wiry and always gave the impression of being full of pent-up energy that might suddenly break out into an explosion of violence.

Was Paul, applying pressure on Anthony to conceal

evidence from the police? Could Paul somehow be mixed-up in whatever had happened to Ian? If he was in charge when it happened – whatever *it* might be – did he feel responsible and want to avoid confessing to whatever mistakes he may have made?

Paige looked very thoughtful as I related all this to him. Then he asked me to go with him to their house that evening. He got me to show the boys my handcuffs and truncheon and to let them try on my helmet. Jenny made us all hot chocolate to drink and then we all sat down together and just talked for about two hours before Paige started to bring the conversation round to the subject of Ian and his friendship with the man in the street.

4 ANTHONY'S STORY

I saw Paul's whole body stiffen as he realised that this was not just a social call, however much we were trying to ingratiate ourselves with the family. He kept darting glances towards Anthony, who seemed about to say something and then closed his mouth abruptly when he saw Paul looking at him. I racked my brains to think of a way of encouraging him to tell us what was on his mind.

Then I had an idea.

'When I was a kid,' I told them, 'I lived in a house with about a dozen other boys and girls. We got up to all sorts of mischief and there weren't many days when one or other of us wasn't in trouble. I didn't like being told off in front of everyone else, so I tried to toe the line, but it wasn't always easy – and sometimes things happened without anyone intending it.'

The boys all quietened down to listen to the story. I guess they liked the idea of a cop confessing to doing something wrong.

'I remember one day a group of us took a ball and a cricket bat out in the garden and had a game. We'd been told *not* to play ball games near the side of the garden next to our neighbour's greenhouse, but it was the best place because it was the only bit of lawn with no trees in it. A boy called Quentin bowled to me and I hit out with all my strength and (unusually for me) I struck the ball square-on and it soared up in to the air … and down right through the top of the greenhouse!'

I had their full attention now. Paul was grinning, in spite of himself. Michael looked interested to know how it would all pan out in the end; and the two younger ones were gazing open-mouthed. I tried to make it sound as dramatic as possible.

'We all scuttled off indoors and made ourselves very busy doing other things. It turned out that the neighbours were away that week, so it wasn't until several days later that we were called to account for the broken pane in the greenhouse roof. Of course, we all denied having anything to do with it, but the ball was a bit of a giveaway, so it was clear that it must have been one of us kids – but no-one could be sure which.'

'So did they punish you all?' James wanted to know. 'That's what the teachers do when they don't know who did something – they keep the whole class in after school.'

'No. My Housefather didn't believe in punishing people for things they might not have done. And he knew that none of us would want to point a finger at one of the others – or to be shown up in front of everyone else.'

'So what *did* they do?' James persisted.

'He called us each in one by one,' I told him.

'And then what?'

'Well, when it was my turn, I went in and stood in front of him, staring at my feet, not knowing what to say.' I paused, hoping to increase the drama.

'Go on!'

'He just sat there looking at me without saying anything. And I stood there feeling more and more uncomfortable and going red in the face … and then, I decided to tell him what happened.'

'Did you grass up the other kids?' Paul wanted to know, interested in spite of himself.

'No. I just told him that I hit the ball over the fence by mistake. And then he asked me what I thought ought to be done about it, and I said that I supposed I ought to pay for the broken glass.'

'But it wasn't just *your* fault,' James put in. 'What about the others?'

'I think that they all – or almost all of them – confessed as well, once they were on their own and not having to speak up in front of everyone else. Anyhow, in the end we were all standing there in front of our Housefather, looking sheepish and wondering what was going to happen to us.'

'And what *did* happen?' Anthony asked.

'He paid for the glass and we all had to go round and apologise to Mr and Mrs Belling for damaging their greenhouse. That was much worse than losing our pocket money would have been, but in the end it wasn't as bad as we were expecting. The Bellings were surprisingly nice about it and showed us round their garden and finished up giving us a bag of plums to take home with us.'

We went on to talk about other things after that, but I could see that Anthony had taken it all in and was thinking about what I'd said. In the end, he plucked up the courage to ask Paige if he could talk to him on his own. I remember Paige looking up at Jenny to check it was all right with her. She nodded and told them to go in the kitchen.

I stayed with her and the other boys and tried to keep them occupied so that they wouldn't sneak off to find out what Richard and Anthony were talking about. I noticed that Paul was looking distinctly uncomfortable and guessed that he knew what Anthony wanted to tell Richard and wasn't very happy about it.

After a few minutes Richard came back in and told Jenny to go and thank Anthony for giving him a big clue to help the investigation. Then he called me and we both headed off. I was burning to hear what the big clue was but Richard wouldn't say anything until he'd called Murdishaw and asked him to meet us at the police station.

It seemed that Paul and Anthony had become curious about what Ian was getting up to and, during half-term, they tailed him and made an interesting discovery. They followed him to a house in a road just round the corner from their own home and saw him being let in by a man whom Paul recognised as the same person that Ian had been meeting in cafés and on street corners.

Wanting a piece of the action, they went up to the door and rang the bell. When there was no answer, they banged on the door and shouted Ian's name through the letter box. Eventually the man, who told them his name was Colin, opened the door and allowed them in. He told them to stop the noise or the neighbours might tell his mother and then he'd be in trouble with her for bringing his friends home while she was out. The boys knew all about getting into trouble with their mother so they promised to be quiet.

Colin took them upstairs to his bedroom, which, according to Anthony was an Aladdin's cave of exciting things. There was a dart board and a pinball machine and Colin taught them all sorts of card games. They had a whale of a time and only went home when Colin told them that his mum would be back soon and she would be angry if she found them there. He made them promise not to tell anyone about coming there in case it got back to his mother.

They went back every day for the rest of the half-term holiday, but after that, Anthony couldn't go because he couldn't bunk off from his Primary School as easily as Ian seemed to do at secondary school. He told Richard that he thought that Paul had started going round to Colin's after school – and even leaving early in order to do so – but he wasn't sure about that. He was pretty confident, however, that Ian was still going round to Colin's house almost every day.

Well, you can imagine the sorts of things that were going through our minds by that stage …

5 FINDING COLIN

While we were waiting for Inspector Murdishaw, Richard got hold of the Electoral Roll and hunted through it for a household in the road where Anthony had told him that the mysterious Colin lived. Eventually he found the house: its residents were a Mr Colin Antrobus and a Mrs Enid Antrobus. As I watched him painstakingly sifting through the list of names and addresses, I realised for the first time the value of mundane and rather ordinary routine tasks in the work of CID. It wasn't all comparing fingerprints and interrogating suspects!

Murdishaw decided that we ought to waste no time in getting round to the house to interrogate Colin. Since I was on hand, he took the two of us with him, which is how I came to be there when the case reached its climax. For a young PC it was very exciting stuff.

The house was in darkness when we got there: it appeared that the residents kept early hours, or else were out. Murdishaw knocked on the door and we all stood there on the path, waiting. Then we heard footsteps on the stairs and a light went on in the hall. There was a fumbling of a key in a lock and the door opened a crack, restricted by a burglar chain. A woman peered out at us suspiciously.

'Mrs Antrobus?' Paige enquired mildly.

The woman nodded but did not speak. Her short hair was brown, just starting to turn grey. Her eyes were dark brown and deep-set.

'I'm Detective Inspector Murdishaw,' the inspector told her, holding up his warrant card. 'I need to speak with your son, Colin. May we come in, please?'

'Can't it wait until the morning?' she wanted to know. 'He's in bed.'

'I'm sorry, but this really is important. We need to speak to him right away.'

'I suppose you'd better come in then,' she grumbled,

releasing the door and opening it just wide enough for us to slip inside. I noticed that she was wearing a dressing gown over pyjamas and concluded that she had already retired to bed – or else was about to do so. She closed the door firmly behind us and beckoned us into a small sitting room at the front of the house. 'Wait here. I'll get him.'

So we sat down and waited. We heard the sound of slippered feet going upstairs and then a mumble of voices above us and finally more footsteps coming back down the stairs. Then, at last, Colin appeared in the doorway, looking round nervously at us, dressed in blue pyjamas and grey slippers. Murdishaw motioned him to sit down, which he did, perching on the edge of his chair as if poised to make a run for it if things turned out badly. His mother followed him into the room and sat down next to him.

For a few moments, we all just sat there, eying one another. Colin was a most unprepossessing young man. He was in his early twenties, thin and scrawny with untidy brown hair and uneven, tobacco-stained teeth. He looked round apprehensively as if trying to work out why we had come and whether he was in trouble.

Murdishaw took out a photograph of Ian and showed it to Colin.

'I think you know this boy,' he said.

'No – no, I've never met him,' Colin protested, becoming even more agitated. 'I've never set eyes on him.'

'Really?' Murdishaw asked in tones of deep scepticism. 'I have witnesses who say otherwise.'

'They must have got it wrong. I tell you I don't know him,' Colin insisted, darting a worried look in the direction of his mother, as if seeking to check that she believed what he said.

Mrs Antrobus grabbed the photograph from Murdishaw's hand and looked at it.

'This is that missing boy, isn't it?' she demanded. 'Your people have already been round here asking us about it. We've already told them that we don't know anything.'

'I know,' said Murdishaw smoothly,' but I'm afraid I don't believe you. Sergeant Paige,' he added, turning to Richard, 'Tell them what young Anthony told you.'

'Mr Antrobus,' Richard began, looking Colin right in the eyes, 'this young man's brother tells me that you used to meet him after school and bring him home here to play pinball and table football. It sounds as if you all had a whale of a time.'

'He's lying,' Colin mumbled. 'I never.'

'Never what?' Murdishaw intervened.

'I never brought kids back here.'

'Anthony says different,' Paige said quietly. 'He says that he's been here too. He told me all about your dart board and your pinball machine and the card games that you taught him. And he gave me a description that fits you to a T.'

'He's making it up,' Mrs Antrobus said sharply. 'He must be. Colin isn't allowed to bring people home while I'm out – tell them Colin!'

'Like Mum says,' Colin said obediently, 'I never brought anyone back here.'

'I see,' Murdishaw said menacingly. 'In that case, you won't mind us having a look in your bedroom, will you? And there won't be any chance of us finding any of Ian's fingerprints up there – on the pinball game, for example?'

'I – I – well OK,' Colin said, sounding flustered. 'I *did* let them come up to my bedroom once or twice, but it was only to play – that's all. I didn't do nothing to them.'

'OK,' Paige said in a conciliatory tone. 'Now, tell us when was the last time you saw Ian?'

'I don't know – last week, I suppose.'

'When last week? Thursday, was it?' Murdishaw asked, naming the day when Ian had gone missing.

'Yes – no – I don't know!'

'Tell us about what happened,' Paige urged gently. 'What time did you meet him, for instance?'

'About two – two-thirty maybe. The usual time.'

'Surely you must have known that he ought to have been at school?' Murdishaw demanded aggressively.

'He didn't like school – he was afraid of the big boys. They kept picking on him. I let him come home with me so he'd be safe. I never hurt him. I never did anything!'

Colin looked round wildly, clearly rattled by Murdishaw's questioning. His mother looked at him with what I took to be a mixture of surprise, anger and anxiety, but said nothing.

'So,' Murdishaw went on, 'you met him in the afternoon – where was that, by the way?'

'On the corner of Jeune Street,' Colin muttered.

'OK. You met Ian there – was it just Ian, or did either of his brothers come as well?'

'Just Ian.'

'And the two of you came back here – is that right?'

'Yes,' Colin nodded, still looking down at a space in front of his feet. 'We went upstairs and played for a bit and then Ian went home – at least, he said he was going home. I can't tell if he really did, can I?'

'And what time was this?' Murdishaw asked.

'About quarter to four, I suppose. He always went in time to get back before his brother.'

'You mean Michael?' Paige asked.

'No – Paul. He didn't want Paul coming here looking for him.'

'I see,' Murdishaw said, leaning closer to Colin and grasping his shoulder to force him to look up. 'So you're telling me that Ian was here last Thursday until about quarter to four and then he went off home and that's the last you saw of him. Is that right?'

'Yes – no – I don't know it was Thursday.'

'He came round here every day,' Murdishaw insisted. 'He never got home on Thursday, so you were the last person to see him.'

'I never said he came *every* day,' Colin protested. 'He never came when my mum was here.'

'Mrs Antrobus?' Murdishaw addressed Colin's mother.

'I work on the buses – different days each week.'

'And last Thursday?'

'I was in work from eight till four.'

'So I reckon,' Murdishaw said, turning to Colin again, 'that Ian was round here that day. I'm right, aren't I?' Aren't I?' He raised his voice menacingly and Colin shrank back.

'Yes, yes,' he admitted. 'He must of been here, like you said – but he went home, like I told you, and I never saw him after that.'

'Now listen here, Colin. DS Paige and I are going to get a search warrant and then we're going to bring a team of forensics officers around to take this place apart and if there's any trace at all of Ian coming to any harm here, we'll find it. So if there's anything you haven't told us yet, now's the time to come out with it, because it'll be a whole lot worse for you if we find you've been concealing evidence – do you understand?'

'I told you – he was OK when he went home. We just played games in my room and then he went.' Colin looked round at us like a rabbit caught in the headlights. I was convinced that he was lying and that he could have told us a whole lot more, but I couldn't help feeling a bit sorry for him.

6 FACING THE INEVITABLE

What followed was, at the same time, very exciting, and painfully predictable. The following day, a team of trained officers descended on the house and went all over it, painstakingly searching for traces of Ian's presence there. It wasn't long before they turned up some minute traces of blood on the carpet runner in the hall, which matched with the blood groups of other members of Ian's family. We didn't have all the sophisticated genetic testing that we use these days, but it was still pretty damning stuff.

I was there when Murdishaw gave Colin the third degree in the hope of getting him to confess and to reveal where he'd put the body. It didn't do any good. Although Colin was clearly terrified, he just kept saying over and over that Ian had left the house alive and that he didn't know how the blood had got on the carpet. I began to wonder if he was telling the truth, because I would have expected a real murderer to have thought up a better story. I mean, it wouldn't have been hard to make up something about Ian accidentally cutting himself, to explain the blood without admitting to having harmed the kid.

We carried on searching the house, pulling everything apart from top to bottom. I remember Richard Paige calling down to me from the loft to bring up a torch. I climbed the ladder and handed up the light. Richard took it and shone it around. Then he whistled gently and called to me to look at the way the dust was disturbed near the trap door that led into the loft.

'It looks as if someone has been up here not all that long ago,' he remarked.

I squeezed up beside him to confirm that there was far less dust on the side where the loft ladder was fixed than on the other sides of the loft access. Richard pulled his bulky form through the aperture and then called down to me to join him. I followed him into the loft and looked round at the dusty rafters. There was no floor up there so we had to be careful not to fall through the plaster into the room below.

Richard slowly directed the torch beam round the roof space, picking out the cold-water tank, a couple of empty tea chests lying on their sides and, finally, a large wooden trunk. Its surface was covered with a layer of dust in which we could see a clear pattern of handprints. Someone must have been up there handling it recently.

We made our way carefully across the loft to the trunk and Richard attempted to lift the lid. It was locked, but it didn't take much to force it open. I'll never forget the moment that Richard raised the lid and leant it against the wall so that we could both peer inside. I'm sure you'll already have guessed what we found there.

The Oxford Times described it as *the mangled remains of twelve-year-old Ian xxx* but it wasn't like that really. Yes, it was Ian's body in there; and yes, it had been crammed into the space, crushing his limbs into a strange unnatural configuration that they could never have had while he was alive; but his face was surprisingly peaceful – almost as if he were asleep – and I felt convinced that the tablecloth that was draped over the body had been put there as a mark of respect as well as for concealment.

Richard and I looked at one another across the trunk. Then he gently replaced the cloth and closed the lid.

'Best get DI Murdishaw up here,' he said briefly.

7 COLIN CONFESSES

When Murdishaw questioned him under caution, Colin broke down and admitted that he had hidden the body, but he claimed that the death had been an accident. According to him, Ian and he had been fooling about at the top of the stairs and Ian had tripped and fallen headlong. When Colin realised that his friend was dead, he panicked and dragged the body up into the loft and hid it in the trunk. He said again and again how sorry he was and repeated over and over again his claim that he had never done any of the boys any harm – or wished any on them.

Personally, I would have been willing to give him the benefit of the doubt, but the jury thought otherwise. The prosecuting counsel painted a picture of a loner, who preyed on young boys and who had killed Ian, either out of frustration when the boy refused his advances (unspecified but assumed to be of the fate-worse-than-death kind) or to prevent him from telling anyone about them.

I remember the trial as if it were yesterday. The thing that struck me most forcefully was the two women watching the proceedings from different parts of the public gallery: Ian's mother, Jenny, and Colin's mother, Enid. They had both struggled to raise their sons alone, and they had both lost them tragically, and now they both gazed down with bewildered expressions on their faces as if unable to comprehend what was taking place.

Colin was found guilty of murder and sentenced to life imprisonment. I've often wondered what became of him, but never made the effort to find out – which is probably the story of Colin's life. His mother disowned him and went to live with her sister down in Weston Supermare to get away from the notoriety; so I doubt if he ever had any visitors or anyone who could be bothered to take the time to get to know him. All very sad, really.

Ian's brothers continued to keep me and my colleagues busy chasing them for minor offences, and Jenny continued to work long hours for low pay in an effort to keep food on the table and shillings in the electric meter. The last I heard, Michael had graduated to training as a bricklayer and Paul had left school and was stacking shelves in the Co-op.

I know that doesn't sound like much of an achievement, when you compare it with the sorts of careers that the kids who come to Oxford as students at the university go on to, but, considering the high unemployment rate at the time, the fact that they were in work at all shows that, for all their faults, they were better kids than most. It's a shame that Ian never got the chance to show what he was capable of .

8 STARTING MY CRIMINAL CAREER

After experiencing a real criminal investigation, I became convinced that I wanted to become a detective. Richard Paige expressed surprise when I confided in him that I was looking to apply to transfer to CID. He said that he thought I fitted in very well to my role as the local Bobby and it would be a shame to leave the community where I seemed to have become trusted and respected. He said some very kind things about how useful it had been that I had already managed to build up a relationship with Anthony and his brothers and that, if it hadn't been for me, he might never have got the story out of him.

I thought this was probably just him trying to make me feel good. Anyway, I'd made up my mind that I didn't want to stay in uniform for my whole police career. Richard was very good about it and gave me lots of tips for improving my application, but I always thought that he had at the back of his mind that I'd missed my real vocation.

The rest, as they say, is history. I eventually got myself selected to move into CID – just about the same time that Richard was promoted to Detective Inspector, as it happens. It may just have been coincidence, but I suspect that he pulled a few strings to get me assigned to a role supporting him, which is how I came to be involved in a murder enquiry at the nurses' home, which turned out to be the most significant enquiry of my whole career. You can read about it in the next section of these memoirs.

DC JOHNS MEETS HIS MATCH

HIS MATCH

(A murder investigation with far-reaching personal consequences.)

1 MY FIRST MURDER

Looking back, 1975 was probably the most significant year of my life, with the most important events kicking off in the autumn, just after the annual 'Sunny Smiles' collection for the National Children's Home had finished. I'd been in CID for just on two years by then, but I hadn't been involved in anything as dramatic as a murder enquiry yet; so when DI Paige told me that we were going over to the nurses' home at the Radcliffe Infirmary to investigate a suspicious death, I was pretty excited. It was pure luck that I was in at the beginning: his favoured sergeant was on leave and I was the only DC on duty that night.

When we got there, we found a group of nurses sitting in their little kitchen with mugs of cocoa. There were four of them: Sister Catherine Spencer, Nurse Jane Bentham, Nurse Elaine Gregg and Nurse Angela Wheeler. They were all in their early twenties and all looking rather shell-shocked.

Sister Spencer was very much in charge. She was the one who had made the call to the police, after another of the nurses in their part of the home had been found dead in her bed that evening. She was a tall, dark-haired woman with deep brown eyes that watched intently as we entered the room. She rose to her feet and signalled to her colleagues to do the same, but Paige waved to them to stay seated. Although in some ways he could be old-fashioned in his outlook, Richard Paige had no sense of his own importance and did not stand on ceremony.

Nurse Bentham was shorter and fairer than Sister Spencer, and less well turned-out. Both nurses had long hair secured in a bun at the nape of the neck but, while Sister Spencer's was neat and tidy, Nurse Bentham's had strands of mousey brown hair dangling from it and several hair grips protruding, as if ready to fall out at any minute. I noticed that nurse Bentham's mug of cocoa had left a brown ring on the kitchen table where it had spilled over while she was drinking it. She looked at us anxiously as if unsure what to expect.

Nurse Gregg was small, lively and garrulous – but perhaps that was just nerves in the presence of the police. She spoke rapidly in a strong Black Country accent, offering to make tea for us and repeating, over and over again, her opinion that it was incomprehensible that anyone should want to kill Susan Parry. As she talked, she took off her nurses' cap and I could see that her brown hair was cut so that the upper layers were shorter than those beneath, in a way that was fashionable at that time. She and Nurse Bentham were both wearing their nurses' uniforms, while the others were in civvies.

Lastly, we come to Nurse Wheeler, who stood out from the group because she was what we used to call at that time 'coloured', which is to say that she was of Afro-Caribbean origin. I later learned that she had come to Oxford from Jamaica only a few months earlier. Her hair was braided across her head in an intricate pattern, in a way that I had never seen before. Her eyes were bright and intelligent. She was of medium height with a curvaceous and beautifully proportioned figure.

Paige started by speaking to the group as a whole. We learned that Nurse Susan Parry had been found dead that evening, when some of her colleagues had gone into her room to investigate why she had not appeared on the ward for her night shift. Sister Spencer had called for help and a doctor had come over from the hospital and examined the body. He had concluded that she had been killed by a stab wound to her chest and had ordered the nurses to call the police.

At this point, Paige stopped the conversation and, after giving the nurses strict instructions to stay where they were, took me to inspect the body. A uniformed constable was guarding the entrance to the bedroom where the remains of Nurse Parry lay. He opened it for us and we went in and looked down at the shape beneath the sheet. Paige reached out and pulled down the covers to reveal a slim, blond figure wearing brushed cotton pyjamas, which lay open at the front, presumably unbuttoned by the doctor who had examined the body. Paige pointed silently at a narrow incision in her chest. A tiny trickle of blood had dried on her skin just below it and there was a small round stain on the sheet beneath. Then he covered up the body again with the sheet and looked round the room.

I followed his gaze, trying to work out what he might be looking for and what he was able to deduce from what he saw. Everything looked very ordinary to me; there was nothing obviously out of place. Paige prowled round, looking at the shelves and peering under the bed.

Suddenly he pounced on a key, which was lying on a small table next to the bed. He picked it up, using a handkerchief so as not to put his own fingerprints on it, and tried it in the door. It turned easily.

'Hmm!' he murmured. 'We seem to have a classic locked-room murder, with our victim inside, the key beside her and the murderer apparently vanished into thin air!'

He replaced the key on the bedside table and went over to the window, craning his neck to see down to the paved area outside, two floors below. Finally, he checked that the window was closed and the catch was fastened.

'Nothing obvious in here,' he said at last, 'but we'll get forensics to go over it in case our killer left any traces behind. Now we'd better get back to those nurses and put them out of their misery. If we take two each we can get their preliminary statements and then let them get off to bed. We'll have a better idea what we really need to know after we get the PM report.'

I started my interviews with Angela Wheeler. She sat at the kitchen table, very calm and business-like, brushing aside my apology for questioning her at such a difficult time. She told me that she occupied the room next to

Nurse Parry's. This gave me an opening to ask when she had last seen the dead nurse.

'Very briefly at the handover on the ward this morning. We're both on male surgical. I'm on "earlies" this week, while she's on nights.'

'I see; and before that?'

'That would be yesterday afternoon. She always goes straight to bed after a night shift and generally gets up sometime in the middle of the afternoon. I met her as I was coming in after my shift. She was on her way out to do some shopping.'

'And over the last few days, did Nurse Parry seem just as normal? She wasn't anxious about anything, as far as you know?'

'Now you ask,' Angela answered, screwing up her face in a very endearing way, like a child with a hard sum to work out, 'she did seem a bit worried these last couple of weeks; but I thought it was just that she was anxious in case she made any mistakes with a patient. She's newly qualified and it is rather daunting for a new nurse to think that we're responsible for people's lives, especially at night, when there's often only one qualified nurse on duty; it's difficult to know sometimes whether a situation warrants getting the on-call doctor out of bed. Susan takes her responsibilities very seriously and I thought she was just nervous about having to make decisions on her own.'

'I see. Now, just for the record, can you describe your own movements from eleven last night to when Sister Spencer called us?'

'Let me see. Well, I was in bed before eleven last night. I got up at six, got dressed, had breakfast and went over to the ward in time for the start of my shift at seven. I was on the ward until half past three, when I came back over here and changed out of my uniform. I nipped out to the shops, then came back and had a cup of tea in the kitchen with Jill Saunders: she's the other nurse who shares this part of the home; you haven't met her because she's on nights.

That would be about half past four.'

'Ah yes. Can I check that I've got it straight? There are six of you sharing this part of the home? And it has a door separating it from the other parts, with a lock that only the six of you have keys for?'

'Well, Mrs Fish, the housekeeper, has a master key and so do Security, but apart from that, yes, only the six of us can open the door.'

'And you each have keys to your own rooms? Do you all keep them locked?'

'When we're out and when we're in bed at night, but I don't think any of us bothers during the daytime if we're in.'

'But Nurse Parry's room was locked when you went to look for her just now: Sister Spencer said that she had to get the master key from the housekeeper's room.'

'Yes. I suppose Susan must have locked it so that no-one would disturb her while she was asleep.'

'The key wasn't in the lock. Do you know where she kept it?'

'She used to put it in her purse when she went out, but I don't know what she did if she locked the door when she was in her room.'

'OK. Now, you were, where, when Nurse Bentham came in looking for Nurse Parry?'

'I was in the passage on my way to the kitchen to make myself some cocoa before bed.'

'And when you met Nurse Bentham you went with her to look for Nurse Parry?'

'Yes. I knocked on the door but there was no reply. Then Elaine and Catherine came up the stairs and Catherine went to telephone to see if Susan might have gone over to the ward after all.'

'And when she came back with the master key, who went in first?'

'Catherine. She opened the door and went in and we all followed her. We all saw that Susan was dead. Catherine checked her pulse and told us to go back and wait in the kitchen. She went down to telephone for help from the hall.'

'And did she lock the door, after you all left?'

'Yes. She said we'd better make sure that no-one wandered in and disturbed anything.'

'I see, so none of you were in the room alone at all?'

'No. We all went in together and came out again together.'

'And Sister Spencer was the first in and the last out?'

'Yes.'

And that was that for the time being. Angela went off to her room and I turned my attention to Nurse Bentham. She was only too eager to tell me everything that had happened that evening in the greatest of detail, interspersing her narrative with her own ideas on what steps the police ought to take in order to discover who had managed to get into her colleague's room and stab her to death as she slept. As I struggled to keep up with her narrative, I wished that I had made more effort to improve my shorthand speed and I was conscious of having to ask my witness to repeat things so that I could be sure that I had got her statements right in my notes. Eventually she ran out of steam and I sent her to her room, telling her to expect to be questioned again at some later date.

As soon as we had finished interviewing the nurses, Paige insisted that we go round to Nurse Parry's home in Bicester to break the news to her parents, despite the lateness of the hour. It was a rule of his that, as the chief investigating officer in a murder case, he should always inform the victim's family himself personally and at the earliest opportunity. This is a rule that I tried to follow myself when I became sufficiently senior to be in charge. It's important for the family to know that they are being treated with respect and that they don't get to hear about their loss through the grapevine – or worse still through the news media – before being officially informed.

As was to be expected, Mr and Mrs Parry found it hard to take in the fact that their daughter had been murdered. They were unable to think of anyone who might have borne her a grudge and were not aware of any arguments or fallings-out between Susan and her flatmates. The only possible help that they could give to the investigation was a vague feeling, expressed by Mrs Parry, that Susan had been uneasy about something that had happened on the ward and had been worrying about whether or not to report it.

2 THE INVESTIGATION CONTINUES

The next day, DI Paige called us all together and briefed his team on the incident.

'On the face of it,' he said, 'we have just five suspects: the other nurses who shared the flat in the nurses' home with Nurse Parry. They – and the housekeeper – are the only people with access to the flat.'

'But someone else could have got hold of a key,' Detective Sergeant Egerton pointed out, always keen to make his presence felt. 'They could have "borrowed" the housekeeper's key – or maybe one of the nurses got a spare key cut for a friend – or, well there are all sorts of ways of getting through a locked door, aren't there, sir?'

'Yes,' Paige conceded, 'that's true; and so we're going to be asking everyone with a legitimate copy of the key to check that it hasn't gone missing and to tell us all about where they keep them and whether anyone else could have got hold of it for long enough to make a copy.'

Egerton smiled complacently, obviously thinking that he had impressed Paige with his perspicacity, but I thought that the Inspector looked rather irritated by the interruption.

'However,' he continued, 'any outsider would be taking a big risk of being noticed by one of the nurses on their way to Nurse Parry's room after they'd got into the flat. I think it's much more likely that our murderer is one of the resident nurses. And there's also the question of the locked room to consider. The murderer must have also had a key to Nurse Parry's room, since the door and window were both locked – and in any case, the room is on the second floor, so an exit through the window is out of the question. It's much more likely that our killer was an insider: one of the nurses who live in that flat. But, since you're so interested in the matter of keys, Egerton, you can take care of that side of the investigation. You need to find out what records are kept of keys to the nurses' quarters. Ask to see the names of everyone who's been given a key to that flat, going back for the last ten years – especially anyone who had a key to Nurse Parry's room as well. She'd only been living there for a few months, so it's possible that the previous occupant still has a copy of the key. Oh! And while you're about it, you might as well do the rounds of all the local key-cutting places to see if any of them remember cutting a key of the design of the flat and/or room keys.'

'Yes sir,' Egerton answered, sounding rather deflated. I guessed that he must have realised that Paige hadn't been impressed by his comment after all.

Paige despatched a team of officers to interview staff at the hospital, beginning with those who worked on the same ward as Susan Parry.

'Find out everything you can about her,' he instructed, 'particularly who her friends were and whether she'd fallen out with any of them recently. And find out if there have been any incidents reported on the ward or any complaints made about any of the nurses – especially about Parry or the others from her flat.'

Once everyone else had left to go about their assigned tasks, Paige turned to me.

'I want you to stay with me,' he said. 'We need to interview the other nurse from the flat and compare what she says with what the others told us yesterday.'

'Yes sir.' I hesitated, unsure whether to voice what was on my mind in case it was presumptuous of me to make suggestions about the conduct of the case; but Paige detected the uncertainty in my voice and urged me to speak up.

'I was just thinking, sir, that it might be better to wait until the afternoon. She was on the night shift last night and will most likely be in bed now.'

'That's a very good point,' Paige said, encouragingly.

'So let's put off going back to the nurses' home until this afternoon. Meanwhile let's have a look at what we've got so far and then there's some work for you to do going through the files to see if any of our suspects has a police record – or if any of them reported any crime.'

We sat down together at Paige's desk. I felt very privileged to have been singled out to work with him and tried my best to create a good impression. I drew up a table showing where each of our suspects had been during the period when Nurse Parry could have been killed.

It looked as if Angela Wheeler was in the clear, because she had been on duty on the ward for the whole time, but we would have to check with the staff there whether she had left at any point and been absent for long enough to return to the nurses' home. Catherine Spencer had a daytime shift in the operating theatres, so she could have slipped in and stabbed Parry before leaving for work that morning. Jane Bentham and Elaine Gregg were both on the late shift that day, so either of them would have had plenty of time to kill their flatmate before going over to the hospital. Bentham worked on the same ward as Parry; so if there was any truth in Mrs Parry's assertion that her daughter was worried about something not right there, that might provide a motive. The fifth nurse – Jill Saunders – was supposedly asleep when Parry was killed, but she could have got up, done the deed and then gone back to bed.

My careful searching of the police records drew a blank. None of the nurses had any sort of criminal past and none seemed to have been the victim of crime either. The only hint of anything dubious was a caution for possession of cannabis issued five years previously to one Graham Lawson, who was now (according to the talkative Jane Bentham) sister Spencer's boyfriend.

3 NURSE WHEELER

Several weeks passed without any breakthrough in the case. It must have been very uncomfortable for the five remaining nurses in the dead girl's residential group. They were all aware that they were under suspicion and they all knew that one of them was almost certainly a murderer. I felt guilty every time we went back to question them further about their relationships with Susan Parry or to cross-examine their colleagues as to their characters and their movements.

Having been brought up by the National Children's Home, I always try to support their fund-raising events. So, when the annual Festival of Queens came around I went along to the Town Hall to watch the pageantry. I suppose I'd better explain what the festival was. Each year Sunday School children and Brownie packs used to raise money for the National Children's home by selling 'Sunny Smiles'. These were pictures of children who were being cared for by the Home. I don't think I was ever considered photogenic enough to be one of those depicted in the little booklets that were distributed all over the country. When all the money was in, the collectors used to come together for a show, at which each church and Brownie pack dressed up a little girl as a queen for the day.

I chose a seat near the back where it would be easy to get out if an urgent call were to come through from Paige. Just as the show was starting, who should come in and sit down next to me but Nurse Wheeler? She looked very attractive in what I took to be her Sunday best: a dark red dress beneath a black coat.

I hesitated before addressing her, thinking that the last thing she would want was to have to talk to someone from the police investigation team; but then I thought that it would be worse if she recognised me and thought that I was following her as part of a surveillance operation. So I spoke to her and I was very gratified that she remembered my name. She told me that she was there with the children from the Sunday School at her church. She'd helped with making the costumes for the queen and her two attendants. We watched the procession of queens walking up the aisle and I congratulated Angela on 'her' queen's costume. Then suddenly the conversation took a more sinister turn.

'It reminds me a bit,' Angela whispered, 'of carnival back home. Only there it's out of doors and rather less restrained.'

'Well, with the British weather, it's rather risky doing things out of doors,' I whispered back, just trying to make conversation. 'And with the British temperament, you would expect restraint!'

'So would you say that West Indians are very different from British people?' Angela asked sharply. It sounded as if I'd hit a nerve, although I couldn't think why.

'No – at least I don't know. I was just joking about the famous British reserve. What are you getting at?'

'A little while ago,' Angela said, speaking slowly and in an undertone, 'I overheard someone saying that West Indians were the sort of people who might very well stab someone to death while they were in bed asleep.'

'What!' I shouted out, unable to help myself. Then I saw people turning to look at us and I forced myself to whisper again. I took Angie by the hand and insisted on going outside where we could talk properly. I wanted to know who had been saying such ridiculous things. Angie didn't want to tell me, but I insisted. I was afraid that she might think that I suspected her of killing her friend – or at least that I might be biased in that direction.

'It was just one of the nursing auxiliaries. I expect she didn't mean anything by it.'

'You don't imagine that the police have that attitude, do you? I mean, surely you must realise that you of all people are not under suspicion?'

'Because I was on the ward that morning? I thought there was a theory that I might have come back during my lunch break.'

I suddenly realised how much pressure our ongoing investigation must have been having on the nurses in Angie's group. I tried to reassure her, forgetting for a moment that I shouldn't be sharing information about the case with anyone outside of the police team.

'No. We had to consider that possibility, but it doesn't work. Look – I shouldn't be telling you this, so you must keep it absolutely to yourself, but the medical evidence shows that she had to have been killed before eleven that morning. And you were on the ward in sight of other staff until half past twelve. So you really are not a suspect.'

I waited for a while to let that sink in before going back to the question of who it was who had suggested that Angie was the murderer.

'Now, I really wish you'd tell me who it was that made that vile accusation against you.'

But Angie wouldn't say.

'No really,' she insisted, 'I couldn't. I'm sure she didn't mean anything by it. It wouldn't be fair for her to get into trouble over something that probably lots of other people were saying – or at any rate thinking – people who didn't get overheard.'

Of course, that only made me see red all the more. I don't know what she must have thought of me, ranting on the way I did.

'What do you mean "other people"? Has this sort of thing happened before?'

'Oh it's nothing,' Angie said dismissively, obviously trying to get me to shut up. 'It's only natural, I suppose, to be nervous of people who are different.'

'But you're not different – not underneath – not in the things that are important! What business have they got saying that you're different?'

'Please Peter,' Angie begged, 'stop worrying about it. It doesn't bother me. It's just one of those things. OK?'

I wasn't convinced, but I could see that Angie didn't want to take things any further. It made me angry that I couldn't go and have it out with the nursing auxiliary – and anyone else who had said similar things – but then I remembered how awkward I felt as a child when one of the teachers heard the other children bullying me over my ginger hair and told them off in front of the whole school. I guessed that Angie was afraid of me making a similar scene.

We decided not to go back to the show, and went for a walk in Christ Church Meadow instead. Angie told me about her family back in the West Indies; about how she was managing to save a little out of her nurse's salary to send back to them to help support a brother with cerebral palsy; and about how much she missed her parents and siblings. I became more and more impressed with her as she talked about her family life and her hopes for the future. All too soon, it was time for us to go back to the Town Hall so that she could escort her Sunday School children back home.

4 An unpleasant incident

The next day, I had another nasty experience of the casual racism that was all too common in those days. I was in the canteen having my lunch with a few of the other younger men. They were all very keen to talk about the upcoming dance and about whom they were planning to take with them. I didn't have anyone to take and was keeping quiet hoping that no-one would ask me about it but, of course, they were determined to know.

'What about you, Johns? Who're you taking?' one of them asked.

'I haven't decided yet.'

'Johns won't have any trouble finding someone,' another of them chipped in, 'what with him having been up at the nurses' home practically every day for the last few weeks. He must know lots of lovely young nurses who'd all be delighted to be asked.'

'I hear one of the ones he's been seeing is a coloured girl. I reckon she'd be a good bet. They can't get enough of it, I'm told.'

'Enough of what?' I asked stupidly.

'Poor Johns!' one of them mocked. 'He's led a very sheltered life. It comes of being raised in an orphanage I suppose.'

'What Constable Adams is saying,' another chipped in, 'Is that coloured girls are usually up for a bit of "how's your father" – especially with a white man.'

'How dare you!' Against my better judgement I flared up, which was, of course, the worst possible thing to do. 'You've no right making that sort of suggestion about someone you haven't even met.'

'Ooh! Hark at him. I reckon Johns is sweet on that coloured nurse!'

'Look at him! He didn't deny it. He fancies her!'

Well, I could hardly stay after that, so I left the rest of my lunch and walked out with as much dignity as I could muster. What I didn't realise was that Paige had been sitting at the next table and had heard everything. He brought up the subject that afternoon, while we were on our way to the hospital to interview the Theatre staff to get more background on Sister Spencer.

'It was brave of you to stand up to Adams and his cronies. I was at the next table. I heard it all. You were right to pull them up about assumptions about people on the basis of race. That's part of being a good policeman: never assume you know what a person's like just because of what they look like, or where they live or what job they do.'

I wasn't used to receiving compliments from senior officers and I didn't know quite how to react. In the end, I think I mumbled something about it not being a matter of bravery.

'I just didn't like what they were saying about Angela,' I explained.

'It's Angela now is it?'

And of course then I realised that I'd given away more than I intended about my feelings about Angie. Paige was obliged to remind me that she was still an important witness in a murder enquiry and any relationship with one of the police investigation team would be completely inappropriate. Then, to my surprise, he went on to say something that made it clear to me that he could read me like a book and had a complete grasp of the situation.

'However, once the enquiry is over,' he said, 'that would be another thing altogether.'

5 LIGHT DAWNS

The following week, we had a breakthrough in the case. We discovered that a former patient on the ward where Nurse Parry worked had put in a complaint, saying that he had been denied pain-relief following his operation. The incident had happened during the period when Sister Catherine Spencer was working there, and it turned out that she was the nurse who had signed for the diamorphine that the patient claimed he had never been given.

That set us off on the path of further investigation of Sister Spencer's private life and in particular her boyfriend, Graham Lawson. We discovered that he had progressed from cannabis to harder drugs and it did not take long to establish that Spencer had been supplying him with diamorphine from the hospital stock. From there, we soon found out that Susan Parry had become aware of an occasion when Spencer had signed for a dose of diamorphine and then 'forgotten' to give it to the patient; and after that everything started to fall into place. Within a matter of days, we had Catherine Spencer and her boyfriend under arrest and it wasn't long before we were in a position to charge her with the murder.

I was pleased that Paige took the trouble to go over to the nurses' home before the news was released to the public, to tell Angela and the others that they were no longer under suspicion. He asked me to go with him, which seemed odd at the time, but I discovered afterwards that it was all part of his plan.

We waited for them in the housekeeper's office. Once they were all there, Paige stood up to address the group.

'I wanted to speak to all of you,' he said, looking round at their expectant faces, 'because I know how difficult it has been for you over the past few weeks, knowing that we have had to treat you as potential suspects in the murder of Susan Parry. I wanted you all to know that you are none of you any longer under any kind of suspicion, and I hope that we shall not need to question any of you again.'

He paused to let the news sink in.

'Please, Inspector,' Jill Saunders asked, 'does this mean that you know who killed Susan?'

'Yes Nurse Saunders, it does. I'm prepared to tell you who it is because the press will no doubt soon get hold of the information, but I'd like to emphasise that anything I say to you now is to be treated as strictly confidential. I'm sure that, as nurses, you understand what that means. Not a word of what is said here to anyone outside this room – and especially nothing to any newspaper reporters. Do you understand?'

They all nodded eagerly.

'Very well,' he continued, 'I can inform you that Sister Catherine Spencer has been charged with the murder of Nurse Susan Parry. I can also tell you – and this is where you must remember not to repeat what you've heard – that she has signed a confession, which makes it clear that she was acting alone. We are therefore not looking for anyone else in connection with this murder.'

There was a short silence while they all considered this news.

'But why did she do it?' Jane Bentham asked at last, voicing what they had all been thinking. 'What had she got against Susan?'

'Sister Spencer had been stealing diamorphine from the ward stock and she was afraid that Nurse Parry had discovered about it. She killed her to prevent her telling anyone.'

'So is Catherine Spencer a drug addict?' Jane asked in astonishment. 'She didn't behave like one. I'd never have guessed.'

'No. She wasn't stealing for herself. She took the drug to give to her boyfriend.'

'But how did she manage it?' Jill asked. 'Drugs like

diamorphine are very carefully monitored. Someone would have noticed that it had gone missing.'

'But it was recorded as having been given to the patients,' Angie broke in. To my surprise, she had already worked out how Spencer had managed to keep her thefts secret for so long. 'She wrote up in the patient notes that she'd administered it, but she just pocketed the phial instead. That's why that patient complained that he hadn't been given any pain killers.'

'That's correct,' Paige agreed. 'She usually only played that trick once with each patient, but she made a mistake with that one and he was left without any pain relief for twelve hours following surgery. When he put in his complaint, it helped us to put two and two together.'

'So let me get this straight,' Elaine said slowly. 'Catherine was stealing diamorphine from the ward and Susan got wind of it and threatened to expose her?'

'I don't think it was as strong as that,' I intervened to stop them thinking that the dead nurse had been a blackmailer. 'As far as we can tell, she didn't make any threats. She thought that Sister Spencer had forgotten to administer the drug to one patient. She talked to her about it and they went and gave it to him. But she was thinking of reporting the incident as a 'near miss' because Spencer shouldn't have written up the notes until after she'd actually given the drug.'

'And Spencer was afraid that, if the incident was investigated, other instances when she'd purloined the drug instead of giving it to a patient might be found out,' Paige continued.

'So then, a few days later, she waited for Susan to come off her night duty and went in and stabbed her to death in her bed, before going on duty herself?' Elaine asked. It looked as if she must have been keeping her own notes and wanted to check what we said against them.

'That's right,' Paige confirmed. 'Working in Theatres, it was easy for her to take away a scalpel from the autoclave one evening and to return it to the hospital the following morning. Her nurse training enabled her to inflict a fatal wound to the heart – something which is not nearly as easy as most people think. She locked the door when she left, using Parry's key, which she replaced on the bedside table when she came in with the rest of you that evening. None of you noticed her putting it there, because you were all too busy looking at the body.'

He looked round at the four faces in front of him.

'Now, that's all I want to say to you. Remember what I said about not passing this on to anyone else. I'm sorry it has taken so long, but I hope that you can all now sleep easy again.'

They got up to go, but Paige called Angie back.

'Nurse Wheeler! If you wouldn't mind staying just for a couple of minutes, Constable Johns has one or two loose ends to tie up and he'd like to ask you some questions.'

He left the room, ushering the other nurses ahead of him. We were left alone. For a moment or two, I couldn't think what to say. Paige hadn't mentioned to me that he was going to do this. I wondered what he was expecting me to say to Angie.

'I wanted to ask you,' I began, still trying to think of something to say. Then I had an idea and tried again. 'There's a police dance next week. I was wondering if you might be willing to go with me.'

Angela looked surprised for a moment and then burst out laughing.

'Is that what the inspector meant when he said you had some questions for me?'

'I don't know, but that's the only question on my mind at the moment.'

'Oh Peter! Of course I'd love to come, but how did inspector Paige know you wanted to ask me?'

'Oh, nothing much gets past him.'

That's about the end of the story, but there was an incident at the dance that I probably ought to tell you about. It shows something of the sort of man Paige is and why it is that we always worked together so well after that.

6 THE POLICE BALL

Paige arrived in the company of a rather overweight and spotty WPC, whom I assumed he had asked out of pity because she couldn't find anyone else to take her. I didn't really want to allow Angela to dance with anyone apart from me: partly because I wanted her to myself, but also because I didn't trust some of my colleagues to treat her properly. Of course, when Richard Paige asked her to accompany him on the floor, I could hardly protest. She told me afterwards about the conversation she had with him as they tripped the light fantastic.

'Why did you want Peter to ask me to the dance?' she asked boldly. 'I mean that *was* the loose end that you said he needed to tie up wasn't it?'

'I didn't want to be stuck here all evening making conversation with WPC Jacobs,' Richard answered in a deadpan voice.

'If you didn't want her company, why did you invite her?' Angie enquired innocently.

'Because I didn't want to have to listen to her for months afterwards sighing and saying what a pity it was that she hadn't been able to come.'

'Wouldn't it have been more straightforward to tell Peter that *he* had to invite WPC Jacobs?'

'No, because then I'd have had Johns going round with a long face, which would have been almost as bad as Pam Jacobs and her moaning. Besides, you'll be good for Peter Johns. He could do with a woman to look after him.'

'Do you mean at the dance or in life generally?'

'Oh generally: it's not good for a policeman to go home to an empty house after spending the day looking at mangled corpses and interviewing victims of assault.'

'What about you then? Peter told me that you were still a bachelor yourself.'

'But I live with my father and grandmother. Thirty-five and still never left home: what d'you think of that?'

'I think your father is a very lucky man.'

'What a very diplomatic answer. I thought you would probably think I was very unadventurous, considering you've travelled half way round the world to be here.'

'I had good reason for coming here. It sounds to me as if you had equally good reasons for staying at home.'

The music reached a conclusion and Richard brought Angie back to join me again. I was with WPC Jacobs, standing close to the bar where a cluster of young men had gathered to collect drinks to take back to their partners. One of them turned to go, lurched sideways and collided with Angie, spilling the contents of his glass down the front of her dress. I immediately recognised him as Adams, the ringleader of the group from the canteen. He was evidently rather drunk.

'Oh look Johns!' he called out, 'your monkey's spilled my drink.'

For a few moments there was a stunned silence in that part of the room. I could hardly believe my ears: surely even Adams must know that this was not the sort of language that he could expect to get away with here? Angie took a step back, looking down and brushing the lager from her dress with her hand to hide her confusion. Pam Jacobs put her arm round her and offered her a paper serviette, which she had picked up from the bar. I recovered enough to step forward with the intention of giving Adams what for, but Richard was too quick for me. He calmly placed himself between us and looked Adams squarely in the face.

'Peter,' he said, without turning his head. 'I think Miss Wheeler would like you to take her outside for a breath of air. The atmosphere in here has suddenly become very unpleasant.'

I knew better than to argue. I took Angela's arm and led her from the room. I found out afterwards that

Richard gave Adams a proper dressing-down in front of everyone. I certainly wouldn't have liked to be in his shoes.

Angie and I went outside into the cool night air and stood on the steps of the hall. I wasn't sure what to do next. I was afraid that this experience might have put her off the idea of going out with a policeman.

'I think I'd like to go home now,' Angela said after a while.

'Yes, of course. I'll walk you back to the nurses' home.'

We set off, walking silently arm in arm.

'I don't suppose he meant any harm,' Angie said. 'I expect it was just the drink talking.'

I thought that it was nice of her to try to give Adams the benefit of the doubt, but I knew she was wrong. Anyway, I was in no mood to let him get away with anything. This incident reminded me too much of something that had happened years previously, and which had made a great impression on me.

'There were a couple of coloured girls in my house,' I told Angie, remembering the scene. 'Sisters. They were five and three when they came. One day, one of the boys made a monkey joke about them. We were all sitting round the table having our tea. I can still see it now. A lot of us laughed at it. Even one of the coloured girls joined in.'

I stopped to think for a minute. Angie didn't say anything, so I went on.

'I never saw my House Father so angry either before or since. He didn't raise his voice; he just spoke in a sort of calm fury. I must have been about ten at the time. I was terrified. He told the boy that his remark was the sort of thing that had sent millions of Jews to the gas chambers. He told the rest of us that anyone who laughed at the joke was just as bad as the boy who made it. He said that for evil to triumph all that is needed is for good people to stand by and do nothing.'

'I think it was a bit hard on a ten-year-old, comparing you to the Nazis.'

'But he was right. That's where that sort of thing starts. I made up my mind, then and there, never to be a party to making fun of someone because of their appearance – after all, I get enough of it myself because of my hair! Anyway, it wasn't being called a Nazi that struck home; it was feeling that he was disappointed in us. I bet that's how Adams is feeling now, with Richard Paige giving him a dressing down. Richard's very well respected in the force.'

'He must be young for an inspector,' Angie commented.

'Yes, but then he lives and breathes the police, so it's no wonder he's a high flyer. I shouldn't think he's ever had a girlfriend or any sort of social life.'

'Thirty-five isn't too old to start,' Angie said, but I could tell she was just teasing me, so I played along with it.

'Oh well, that's it then!' I declared, as if I were taking her seriously. 'If I'm in competition with old Richard I might as well give up now. Shall I go back and fetch him so that he can take you home?'

'Don't be silly, Peter,' Angie giggled, squeezing my arm. 'I much prefer redheads – didn't I tell you?'

OUR BERNIE

(My explanation of how we got it together.)

1 FIRST IMPRESSIONS

I remember the first time I met Our Bernie. Angie and I were on duty at the door of our church, welcoming people as they arrived and handing out notice sheets. At least – Angie was on duty and I was standing with her because I saw that as preferable to sitting down in the church on my own and being approached by members of the congregation trying to show an interest in one of the young people.

As I say, we were standing there on the steps when this girl came along. She was a bit shorter than Angie and looked very young – partly because her hair, which was a sort of nondescript mousey-brown, was braided in two plaits, which hung down her back and made her look like a refugee from St Trinian's. She wore national health glasses and no makeup. I judged her to be about sixteen and wondered what had brought her to church on her own without any parents.

Angie greeted her warmly – newcomers always get an especially warm greeting, particularly if they are young – and asked her if she'd been before. Angie was always much better at that sort of thing than I am. Before long, she had found out that the youngster was called Bernadette Fazakerley, but preferred to be known as Bernie; that she was a postgraduate student (which made my estimate of her age at least five years out); that she was studying for a mathematics degree; that she lived in a rented house not far away; and that she hailed from Liverpool. (That last piece of information was obvious the moment she opened her mouth!)

Before she went to sit down, leaving Angie free to speak to the next arrivals, we also knew that Bernie had been brought up to attend the catholic church and the salvation army citadel in equal proportions, that her father worked in the docks and that her mother was dead. I marvelled at Angie's ability to get people to talk about themselves and wished that I were as effective when questioning witnesses.

When it was time for the service to start, Angie and I crept in at the back and Angie made a beeline for Bernie, who was sitting on her own. We sat down next to her and she smiled at us rather absently. I got the impression that she might have preferred to remain alone.

There was tea and coffee served after the service. At first Bernie looked as if she were intending to go home, but Angie pressed her gently to stay and we all trooped through to the church hall and joined the queue. Betty Appleby, who was serving, asked Bernie her name and where she was studying and then, as Bernie put out her hand to accept the biscuit that Betty offered her, she commented on the engagement ring that Bernie was wearing.

'Who's the lucky man then?' Betty asked cheerfully.

Bernie immediately coloured and looked extremely uncomfortable. After a second or two she recovered enough to say, 'he died.' And that was that. Betty looked very taken aback and then she looked as if she were about to ask some more, but Angie, noticing Bernie's discomfiture, intervened.

'Bernie,' she said firmly, taking her by the arm. 'I'm sorry to interrupt but you really must see the artwork that my Junior Church group did last week. Come through here and I'll show you.'

2 SECOND THOUGHTS

After that, I suppose I shouldn't have been surprised when a couple of weeks later Angie invited Bernie for Sunday lunch at our house after church. I wasn't best pleased, to be honest, because I preferred to have Angie to myself whenever we were lucky enough both to have a day off. With her being a nurse and me being a police officer, we could sometimes go for several weeks without our off-duty coinciding.

I noticed that Bernie no longer wore her engagement ring. Angie told me afterwards that she had continued to wear it as a way of signalling that she did not consider herself available, but that the incident at the church had made her decide that it was better to appear unattached than to provoke enquiries about her fiancé.

At first, I didn't like Bernie much. She seemed to me to be rather loud and aggressive – which I now realise was a defence mechanism to avoid evoking people's pity. She didn't like to talk about herself and it was some months before she confided to Angie what had actually happened to Stephen. It gave me quite a jolt when I heard that he had killed himself only a few weeks before they were due to get married. It somehow changed my ideas about Bernie completely. I couldn't imagine how I would have felt if Angie had committed suicide.

I probably ought not to have done, but I got hold of the police file on Stephen's death and read up about it. I wanted to know if there was any reason why he had done such a strange thing – especially at a time when he should have been blissfully happy, looking forward to his wedding day. Not that the file told me much. The one thing that was completely clear was that no one at all had seen it coming or could think of any reason for what he did.

I was surprised to find that Bernie hardly featured at all. There was a lot of concern for Stephen's parents, but Bernie seemed to be lumped together with a list of also-rans: fellow-students and staff from his college who had been interviewed in case they could throw any light on his state of mind. It didn't seem to have occurred to anyone that the boy's fiancée might have been in need of any support. I like to think that we would handle things better these days.

Having said that, you can take a horse to water but you can't make it drink. I can't honestly see Our Bernie submitting to counselling if it had been offered to her – that would have been too much like admitting that she couldn't cope on her own.

We realised years later that our friend Jonah Porter (of whom you may have heard elsewhere) had actually been involved in a minor way. He was the first police officer on the scene (as a humble PC – insofar as Jonah was ever a humble anything – before making the transition into CID) and was responsible for keeping the public away while they cleared up the mess. He confessed to having found it tremendously exciting because it was his very first suspicious death and he had visions of it turning out to be a murder enquiry. As it was, it was simply a "routine" student suicide.

Jonah was appalled when I told him how Bernie had been side-lined in the investigation and I could see that he thought of himself as one of the people who didn't think to do anything for her. There was a time when I would have enjoyed seeing his discomfiture – I used to think he was too full of himself and needed taking down a peg or two. But, since his disabling injury, I've got to know him better and I realise that he's quite vulnerable in his own way.

Since Jonah would be mortified to think that I'd changed my opinion of him because I feel sorry for him – although, of course I do (as anyone would) and he will just have to like it or lump it – and he will quite probably read this, I'd better add that I don't mean that I like him better now that he is dependent on us in so many ways. It's simply that having him living with us has given me the chance to get to know the real Jonah Porter and not just the super-efficient DCI. And part of that is realising that, if you believe in your own abilities as much as Jonah does, every small mistake feels like an abject failure, because you think that you ought to have got it right.

But I digress. This was supposed to be a story about Our Bernie and how Angie and I got to know her.

In fact, I don't think I did get to know Bernie until a few years later. She and Angie were soon thick as thieves. I think Bernie was the first really close friend that Angie made since coming to Britain. Of course, she had plenty of friends amongst the nurses at the hospital, and the people at church were all very friendly towards both of us, but Bernie was the first person (apart from me) that Angie came to rely upon and to confide in. I have to admit to being a bit jealous at first because I didn't really think she ought to need anyone except me!

Anyway, Bernie became a part of our life and she often came round for meals or I would find her sitting with Angie when I got home if Angie's shift finished earlier than mine. To be fair to her, she always made herself scarce as soon as I arrived, so that we could be alone together. And then, it wasn't long before we had something much more significant to think about – Angie was pregnant and we started to look forward to a new stage in our family life.

3 NOW WE ARE THREE

Hannah was born on 22nd September 1980. I think for Angie it was quite hard not to have her own mother around for such a momentous occasion and we certainly soon discovered that not having any grandparents living locally – or even on the same continent – was a big disadvantage when it came to childcare. We also discovered that, while two may be able to live as cheaply as one, the cost of having a third, small and demanding, member of the family changes everything for the worse in financial terms.

It became clear that Angie would have to go back to work at the end of her six week's maternity leave and that she would need to work full-time and to do as many out-of-hours shifts as she had been doing before – if, that is, we were to continue to send some cash home to her family in Jamaica every month. It was at that point that we really started to appreciate Bernie's contribution to our family life. At least – to be honest – I didn't think much about it myself. I just got used to finding Bernie there looking after Hannah when I got home. That might have been two or three times a week, depending on Angie's and my shift patterns. She would always slip away once I was there to take over, so I still didn't really get to know her at that stage. I do remember worrying that Hannah might pick up a Liverpool accent and wondering what they would make of it when she started school!

Then, when our son Eddie was born, Bernie naturally took a similar role in his upbringing; but Eddie needs a chapter to himself …

4 COME IN NUMBER FOUR!

It came as a terrible shock to Angie and me when we got a letter from the school asking us to come in to discuss Eddie's attendance record. We knew that he'd found the transition from First to Middle school difficult, but we had no idea that, by year eight, he had started simply staying away on a fairly regular basis.

After we'd had what felt to us like a dressing-down from the head teacher, we came home and talked to Eddie about his truanting. Angie tried to reason with him, emphasising how important it was to study hard and get good qualifications, and I told him about the law that required us to see that he attended school. I don't think either of us made much impression on him. He simply wasn't interested in what school had to offer. We found out much, much later that he was also being bullied, but he didn't let on about that at the time.

We tried to arrange our shifts so that one of us could accompany him to the school gate every morning and see that he actually did go in. We thought that at least then he would find it more difficult to bunk off for whole days at a time. The trouble was we both had jobs that often needed us to be flexible about our hours. So Angie asked Bernie to help out, which she did willingly. That was probably the point at which I started to get to know her better through all those mornings when she would be at our house before breakfast so that I could get off to work knowing that she would see Eddie safely off to his lessons.

The start of Eddie's problems almost exactly coincided with the start of Bernie's relationship with my boss, DS Richard Paige. In fact, I remember that the summons from the head came through on the very day Bernie was moving back into her own house after spending the summer staying with him, following the fire. (You can read all about that elsewhere.) That was another factor that made me take more of an interest and stop viewing Bernie as just one of Angie's friends from church.

I think Eddie must have found it easier to talk to Bernie than to me and Angie. Probably he thought she was less old-fashioned and stuck-in-the-mud. He probably also realised that she was less likely than me to go off the deep end if he complained about the school or about the way some of the other boys were treating him. However, for quite a while we didn't really see much improvement in his behaviour. Although he now attended school in body, his reports and the comments from his teachers at parents' evenings suggested that his mind was very much elsewhere.

We even started to worry that he might be getting into drugs. Every evening he would disappear up into his room and showed no interest in being part of family activities. He had one real mate – a boy who lived in the next street who had been his friend since they started nursery together. He had a computer in his bedroom – something that was still relatively unusual in those days, at least amongst our acquaintances – and they used to spend hours together there playing games. Angie and I thought it was a waste of time and that they would be better doing something active like swimming or playing football in the park, but at least it kept them off the streets.

As Christmas approached, Bernie came to us with a proposition. She wanted to help Eddie to build himself a computer. I thought it was a ridiculous idea, but eventually she managed to convince us that it was both feasible and potentially useful for him in his future career. Of course, she was right and I was wrong. That proved to be the turning point for Eddie. I don't know whether it was having an adult spending time with him doing something that interested him, or discovering that he was actually good at something, or realising that he might be able to spend his working life doing something that he actually enjoyed, but all of a sudden his whole attitude changed.

We'd started to despair of him ever getting any decent

GCSEs. However, by the time he started in year ten, he'd begun to put a real effort into his schoolwork – especially the subjects that Bernie told him he's need to do well in if he wanted to do Computer Science at university – and in the end, he managed some really impressive grades. In fact, in some subjects he did better than Hannah, who had been such a steady dependable girl and never caused us any worries school-wise.

5 FIVE DAYS OF HELL

I suppose it must have been a year or more later that Richard managed to get himself caught up as one of the hostages in a terrorist siege. I don't know all the details myself, because it was all under the supervision of Special Branch and information was distributed on a "need-to-know" basis, which seemed to mean that no one was allowed to know anything! And what little I do know is probably still supposed to be kept under wraps, so I'll gloss over all of that. The important thing, from the point of view of Bernie's story, is that he was out of circulation for five days with pretty well no news coming through about what might be happening to him.

At that point I had no idea how close Bernie and Richard had become until she rang that Monday wanting to ask Angie if by any chance Richard might be away on police business with me and did she know when he might be likely to get back. Angie handed her over to me and I tried to explain without giving away any official secrets – which was pretty difficult. In the end, I told her about the hostage situation – just the bare fact that Richard was being held – and swore her to utmost secrecy. After that there was nothing much any of us could do except wait.

Eddie was extremely scathing when he realised that I hadn't been aware of the arrangement that Bernie and Richard had, whereby she entertained him to dinner (only she *would* insist on calling it "tea") on Mondays and Thursdays, and she would go round to his place on Tuesdays and Fridays. As I'm sure Jonah would be delighted to point out, it just goes to show how much good I am as a detective! I *had* noticed how Eddie never went round to Bernie's for help with his homework on Tuesday or Friday and how Richard always tried to get away from work on time on those days too, and yet I never put two and to together.

Angie, of course, knew a whole lot more about what

was going on than I did, but I think Eddie probably had a better grasp of the situation even than she did. He'd been round there on lots of Mondays and Thursdays getting help with knotty problems in maths and physics, and he'd seen them together, which neither of us had.

Angie invited Bernie to come round to our place on Tuesday evening, but she turned the offer down and made it pretty clear that she intended to see this thing through on her own. Angie debated with me whether she ought to go round to check that Bernie was OK, but she wasn't sure whether that might just make her more reluctant to accept help later if the worst were to happen. In the end, Eddie took charge. He declared that he had some chemistry homework that was completely impossible and he would have to get Bernie's help that very evening because it was due in the next day. Without another word, he was off out of the house and round to her place.

I was very proud of him in those five days. You don't expect sensitivity from a fourteen-year-old boy, but he showed a remarkable level of understanding of how Bernie must have been feeling. All his teachers must have decided to set particularly challenging homework that week, judging by the length of time he spent going thorough it with Bernie each evening! The first night, Angie went round to fetch him back after a couple of hours, worried that he might be overstaying his welcome, but she came back convinced that he was doing her good.

In the early hours of Friday morning it was all over. I don't know the details, and couldn't tell them to you if I did, but news came through that the siege was lifted and all the hostages had been freed safe and sound. Richard reappeared in the office around ten-thirty, looking tired and harassed but otherwise unscathed. My first thought was for Bernie. I accosted Richard as soon as I could get him in the privacy of his own office and asked him if he'd been in touch with her yet. I could hardly believe it when he looked back at me as if I had gone off my head. I honestly believe that it had never occurred to him that she might have been worried about him.

I did my best to impress upon him the importance of letting her know at once that he was safe and then packed him off with instructions to go straight round to see her. I told the rest of the team that Richard was taking the rest of the day off to recuperate after his ordeal, and I rang Angie to make sure that she prevented Eddie from calling round on Bernie that evening. And we all expected that it wouldn't be long before Richard and Bernie admitted publicly that they'd fallen for one another.

6 Six months of suspense

I suppose it was, by their standards, quite a whirlwind romance, which culminated in their getting married six months or so later. But it wasn't at all the straightforward business that Angie and I anticipated.

I was half expecting Richard to announce their engagement when he came into work the Monday, after being released from captivity. But he made no mention at all of Bernie or of the fact, which Eddie had imparted to us, following his own personal surveillance operation, that Richard's car had spent the whole weekend from Friday afternoon to Monday morning parked outside Bernie's house. The only perceptible difference that the events of the previous week appeared to have made to Richard was that he seemed somehow serene and confident in a way that he never had previously. It's hard to describe, because it's not as if he used to be jumpy or had ever lacked confidence in his own abilities, but there was definitely something there that he hadn't had before. Looking back, and knowing so much more about him, I think he had at last started to believe that it might be possible for someone to really care about him for himself.

Angie and I had a frustrating time over the next few months as we watched the romance – if you can describe it as that – between Richard and Bernie going nowhere fast. Bernie was Angie's best friend and she naturally wanted to see her settled happily in a permanent relationship. Although Richard was my boss, he had also become a good friend of mine and I'd often thought how sad it was that he had never appeared to have any sort of life outside of his job. So we were both rooting for them to get it together and were both disappointed that it was taking them so long.

They continued to share meals together four days a week – and I rather fancy they often spent most of the weekend together as well – but, as far as we could tell, through judicious spying – they were always both safely back in their own separate homes each night. And Richard continued to come alone to all those formal events for senior officers that included an invitation to bring a partner.

I don't know whether Richard would ever have got round to popping the question if it hadn't been for an incident that provided the final push for him into realisation that, whatever he might think, someone did actually care about him.

You may remember that Bernie had been engaged before – as an undergraduate – and that her fiancé had killed himself. The upshot of all that was that Bernie had formed a close relationship with the boy's parents, Stan and Sylvia Corbridge. They lived in Newcastle-upon-Tyne – way up in the North East – which meant that Bernie only got to see them once or twice a year. Both of her own parents were dead and they had no other children, so Bernie saw herself as having some sort of filial responsibility for them. She'd mentioned to Angie years previously that she'd like to find a job up there so that she could move closer to them. I think that, as well as just for friendship's sake, she felt that she had an obligation to look after them in their old age, when it came.

Anyway, there was this professorship advertised at the university up there and Bernie applied. It wasn't the first time she'd tried, but this time she was shortlisted. I remember her being very nervous of going to the interview because there was so much hanging on it. Angie was round at Bernie's when the phone call came through offering her the job, and she told me about it afterwards. Bernie went very white and then flushed red in confusion and said, in a very small voice, 'I'm sorry. I've decided I don't want to leave Oxford after all.'

According to Angie, there was quite a long conversation in which the person at the other end of the line appeared to be trying to persuade Bernie to change her mind. However, she held her ground, while apologising profusely for wasting their time, told them that her decision was for personal reasons and, a minute or two later, put the phone down.

Well! You can imagine what conclusions Angie drew from all that. I wasn't sure whether to be pleased that she wasn't going off and leaving Richard or annoyed that she'd had to give up both a step up in her career and the opportunity to move closer to Stan and Sylvia, who were such old friends and probably more deserving in many ways than Richard. Richard was already old enough to retire from the Police Service if he had a mind to; so why couldn't he move up to Newcastle with her? (Not that I wanted either of them to go, but it seemed the obvious solution.)

The final straw for me came later that week, when Richard and I were at lunch in the canteen. I was trying to make small talk and I happened to ask about what he was doing at the weekend. He told me he was taking Bernie out to cheer her up after missing out on the Newcastle job.

She hadn't told him, had she? She hadn't told him that she'd been offered the job, because she didn't want him to know that she'd turned it down in order to stay in Oxford with him. All she'd said to Richard was that she wouldn't be moving to Newcastle after all, and he'd naturally assumed that her application had been unsuccessful.

I wasn't sure which of them I was most angry and frustrated with: Bernie for not being honest with Richard for fear of hurting him by making him feel guilty that he'd messed up her career, or Richard for not being able to see how much she cared about him. Why couldn't he have told her before the interview that, if she got the job, he'd move up there with her? I'm sure that's what he would have wanted to do – except that, I suppose he would have thought it was presumptuous of him to imagine that she would want him to!

Anyway, something snapped and I gave him a right

rollicking over his denseness in not seeing what was going on. I spelled out to him the fact that Bernie had turned the job down, even though the university were very keen to get her to come. I told him in words of one syllable that she had decided to stay in Oxford in order to be with him. He looked sort of bewildered and didn't seem able to believe me. Then he went and shut himself up in his office with strict instructions that he wasn't to be disturbed, because he had an important report to write.

About half an hour later, he came out and headed off down the stairs without speaking to anyone. He was back again after an hour or so, still saying nothing, but there was something about him that was different. The important report was apparently not important any more and he spent the rest of the afternoon doing the rounds of all his senior officers, checking how they were progressing with the work in hand and offering advice. When it came to me, he called me into his room and closed the door. I waited for him to open the conversation, but he didn't seem to know how to begin, so I started on an account of the spate of burglaries that I'd been investigating in Botley.

He showed polite interest, but clearly wasn't really listening. After I'd had to repeat what I'd said a couple of times, he apologised and then, with apparently a great effort, blurted out that he and Bernie were getting married and would I be his Best Man? Of course, I was delighted – and so was Angie when Bernie told her later that day. We both hoped that they would have a long and happy marriage. Obviously it couldn't be as long as we might have wished for, because Richard was nearly twenty years older than Bernie, but he was very fit for his age and we never for a moment thought that he would be killed within a couple of years – but that's another story.

7 SEVEN DAYS OF HEAVEN

We had quite a time persuading Bernie and Richard to take a proper honeymoon. Their first idea was to get married on Saturday and for Richard to be back in work on the Monday. However, I eventually forced him to recognise that such a course of action would be sure to encourage all sorts of silly banter about the wedding night and so on – much better to give people a few days to get it all out of their system in his absence. It was July, so Bernie, being an academic, was completely free of work commitments, which meant that it was ridiculous not to go away and have some time alone together, but they somehow both seemed reluctant. I almost wonder whether they weren't sure that they would find enough to talk about for a whole week.

In the end, Stan and Sylvia Corbridge (the friends whose son Bernie had so nearly married twenty years earlier) took them in hand and organised the rental of a small cottage out in the wilds of Northumbria. Bernie agreed at once – mainly because they could call in to see Stan and Sylvia while they were there and it would give Richard a chance to get to know them properly – and Richard, in his usual self-effacing way, just went with the flow.

Naturally only Bernie and Richard know what went on during those seven days, but I do know that they only called in on the Corbridges once (on the way home to Oxford) instead of the 'two or three times' that Bernie had proposed. So I rather fancy they found more to do alone together than they'd imagined!

8 EIGHTEEN MONTHS LATER

It's hard to believe that Bernie and Richard had less than two years together from his, belated, proposal of marriage to his untimely death. To Angie and me, it felt as if they had always been a couple. It was something of a surprise to me, after having known Richard for so long and having assumed that he preferred a solitary life, that it so soon became impossible to think of seeing them apart (except during working hours, of course). And that made it all the harder to come to terms with Richard falling to his death only weeks before he was due to retire.

Retirement had been something that had hung over Richard for several months. It was quite clear that he didn't want to go, but equally clear that he was being eased out and that the most he could hope for was to be permitted to continue in some sort of "safe" desk job. For someone who had always been very hands-on, that would have been intolerable, so he had agreed to go gracefully rather than to fight on against the inevitable.

Bernie, of course, being nearly twenty years younger – and that was something else that made it so surprising that they became so inseparable once they had admitted to one another that they did actually care for each other – would continue working; so Richard started to think about how he could fill the empty days. I know that it preyed on his mind that he might become difficult to live with if his mind was no longer occupied with his job. Maybe that was what made him careless and take risks that he would normally have avoided.

Anyway, for whatever reason, he took it upon himself to chase an escaping suspect across the roof of one of the colleges. The man turned on him in an attempt to escape down the stairs up which they had come, and in the struggle Richard fell to the ground and broke his neck. He died in the ambulance on the way to hospital. Bernie arrived too late to say goodbye – or to tell him the news that she was carrying his unborn child.

I was glad to have been there when he fell – although I can never forgive myself for not having arrived a few minutes earlier and been able to prevent it – and to have spoken to him as he lay there waiting for the ambulance to arrive. Bernie was uppermost in his mind and he gave me a message for her: "tell Bernie I'm sorry." We're still trying to work out exactly what he meant.

9 NINE DAYS WONDER?

Bernie was surprised that so many people turned out for Richard's funeral. Although he'd never attended, pretty much everyone from the church that Bernie and Angie belonged to was there, and there was a big police contingent. My biggest surprise was seeing DCI Jonah Porter in the congregation. He had been a junior colleague of mine in the old days, long before Bernie met Richard, but he'd moved away to South Oxfordshire to take up an inspector's post and I hadn't seen him for years. He's the same age as Bernie, which means seven years younger than I am. However, he was much better at getting himself noticed – and to be fair, much better at making those unexpected leaps of imagination that can sometimes be crucial to solving a case – so he got promoted ahead of me. He thinks I resented that, but I didn't really, even though in the early days I taught him a lot about basic investigation work.

Anyway, he turned up from nowhere at the funeral and asked me to introduce him to Bernie. Basically, he was curious to see what sort of woman old Richard had taken up with after having been a bachelor for so long. Well, whatever else, he couldn't complain that Bernie was ordinary! I could see he hadn't been expecting a loud-mouthed scouser or an Oxford don – and certainly not both rolled into one! However, Jonah is never wrong-footed for long, and soon they were getting on like a house on fire. It rather annoyed me at the time to see young Jonah even managing to outshine me with one of my (or rather Angie's) oldest friends.

After Bernie went off to circulate among the guests again, Jonah got me to promise that I'd let him know when the baby was born – so he could send a card. At least, that's what he said he was going to do. I never expected him even to bother with that, but I sent him an email when the baby arrived all the same, seeing as I'd promised.

It never occurred to me that this would be the start of something that eventually changed all our lives forever.

10 TEN P.M.

It must have been pretty miserable for Bernie during the six months following Richard's untimely death. She felt desperately guilty that she had not told him that there was a baby on the way, and she worried that she might not manage to convey to the baby that he/she had a father to be proud of. I did what I could, but Angie was much better than I was at helping. Of course, it was easier for her because there were so many things that she could share with Bernie about the whole process of becoming a mother, which if nothing else must have helped to keep her looking forward instead of brooding on the past.

Anyway, eventually little Lucy arrived. Of course, Bernie couldn't do anything the conventional way. When she went into labour, she rang us at home, as we'd agreed, but I was out on a case and Angie was doing an extra shift because they were short-staffed. She and Angie had arranged that Angie would be there at the birth as what they call in obstetric circles a "birthing partner". Basically, it's someone to hold the expectant mother's hand and do all the things that the father is expected to do if he's present. She got through to Eddie who generously volunteered to drive her to the hospital. Since he'd only passed his test a couple of weeks previously, Bernie very sensibly declined the offer.

Of course, what most people would have done under the circumstances would have been to call a taxi – or even an ambulance – but Our Bernie couldn't be doing with any of that! She reckoned up that it was "only a couple of miles" and decided to walk it. Admittedly, she'd been cycling into college every day right up until the end of Hilary term, which was only about six weeks before D-day, and hadn't slowed down noticeably in any other respect either in the run up to becoming a mother, but I'm glad Angie had showed less independence of spirit when our two were imminent.

She made it without incident and went to reception to check herself in. it was only when her waters broke while they were taking down her details that it dawned on her that maybe she'd taken a bit of a risk. By that time it was near the end of Angie's shift and one of the nurses helpfully contacted her to ask her to come straight to the labour ward, so it wasn't long before things got back on to the pathway that we'd planned.

When I got home, I found Eddie in a state of great agitation. Anyone would have thought that he was the expectant father! There was nothing for it but for the two of us to go straight off to the hospital to get the latest news. Everyone was very kind and they found us seats in the waiting room and plied us with cups of tea, although I could see they were wondering who on earth we were. Eddie was like a cat on a hot tin roof and I was starting to get anxious myself as a result. I tried to remember how long it had taken for Hannah to be born – far longer than I had imagined it would be, I remembered, but that was not a very useful measure. Childbirth was more dangerous when you were older, wasn't it? If something had gone wrong, how long would it be before anyone would tell us?

Of course, all our fears were groundless and by about ten that night Angie emerged carrying the new baby to show us. I was surprised at how entranced Eddie seemed to be at her little hands and tiny screwed-up face. It isn't something you associate with teenage boys!

11 A NEW FIRST LADY

Bernie asked Angie and me to be Lucy's godparents. Of course, we were delighted to agree, and that marked the beginning of one of the most fulfilling relationships in my life. I have to admit to being extremely fond of Lucy – something that started almost from the very beginning. I feel a bit guilty that I somehow managed to find more time for her than I ever had for my own two kids. I suppose that by the time Lucy came on the scene I was settled in my career – or rather I'd given up any idea of progressing further than I'd already come and was content to leave striving to get oneself noticed by the hierarchy to more ambitious, younger officers. Maybe I was also more confident in my own abilities and so didn't feel the need to justify my existence by putting in excessive hours – or maybe I realised that I was not indispensable and was more willing to delegate.

Though I say it myself, it wasn't long before Lucy started making it plain that I was her favourite human being – apart from her mother, of course! Angie used to joke that Lucy was starting to displace her in my affections and to refer to her as my "other woman"!

Angie and Bernie, of course, were still the best of friends and Angie was like a second mother to Lucy. Eddie also took a great deal of interest in Lucy and became something between a big brother and a favourite uncle. Eddie continued with his preparation for university and, in due course, with Bernie's help, he went off to study Computer Science at Manchester – which Our Bernie told us was the best place in the country, not even excepting Oxbridge. Everything seemed to be going along very nicely, until a few weeks before Angie and I were due to celebrate our silver wedding.

But that's another story and will have to wait for another chapter.

12 SECOND TRAGEDY

It was 23rd May 2003. It was just five weeks before our Silver Wedding. Unknown to me, Bernie and Angie had arranged to drive over to Abingdon to visit the jeweller's where we bought our wedding rings, with the intention of choosing something special for me to mark the occasion. But none of those things happened, because something else interrupted the smooth running of our lives. Something that changed them forever.

I went into work as usual, leaving Angie at home, because it was one of her off-duty days that week. Everything was just as usual until suddenly I was aware that Chief Superintendent Adrian Fuller had walked into the room and was trying to attract my attention. His face looked grim and I somehow knew that there was something very wrong. I suppose he had the look that policemen put on when they are about to break bad news. I must have seen it dozens of times, but it had never applied to me before.

'Your friend, Bernadette, telephoned,' he began, and I immediately thought of Lucy. Had she had an accident? Why had Bernie called the Chief Super instead of speaking to me direct?

'I'm afraid it's your wife,' he went on. I don't remember what he said next, everything is a blur from that point onwards. I vaguely recollect being driven home to find the street full of emergency vehicles and then going inside and seeing Angie's body lying on the kitchen floor in a pool of blood. And then someone led me out again and put me into a car. I remember sitting on the back seat, with Lucy next to me, stroking my face with her hand and trying to comfort me. And then, one thing I remember quite clearly was her asking whether Angie was dead and Bernie answering her, very matter-of-fact.

This is about Bernie, so I won't go into the investigation into Angie's murder or the way it remained an unsolved mystery for years, until Jonah Porter came along and reopened the case. You can read about those things in other books, because Jonah told the whole story in an interview with a television reporter.

For me the only important thing was that the woman with whom I'd shared my life for more than a quarter of a century was no longer there. And our two children – young adults now, of course – no longer had a mother. Bernie was incredibly kind. She didn't intrude, but she made it clear that I was welcome at her home any time I chose to turn up.

And she understood when it got too difficult for me going on living in the house where Angie and I had been so happy, which had been spoilt by the memory of that dreadful picture of her lying on the kitchen floor, covered in her own blood. Once Eddie had gone back to Manchester to start his final year at university, I more or less moved into her spare bedroom – although I made a point of moving back to the family home whenever one of the kids decided to come down to check that "poor Dad" was OK.

Of course, at that stage it never crossed my mind that there was any possibility that I might marry again. Nobody, nobody at all could ever replace Angie.

13 FAMILY OF THREE

If anyone asks her why she married me, Bernie always says, 'Because he was there!'

You can read her account of how it happened elsewhere. Here's an extract of her conversation with Jonah about it.

'A month or two after Eddie left for Jamaica, Peter came for a weekend and never quite got round to going back – apart from moving back into the family home whenever Hannah paid a flying visit to check that Dad was OK. I imagine that lots of people made wild, unfounded assumptions about the actual sleeping arrangements, but he really did occupy the spare room for over two years. As anyone with an ounce of common sense would understand, he was far too devoted to Angie's memory to be in the least tempted to do anything else.'

'So what changed?'

'Nothing really. But I suppose it was just a matter of time. One evening Peter came downstairs after putting Lucy to bed and I made some remark about how much she liked having him reading her bedtime story. We were sitting together on the settee in the living room. He said something along the lines of: he supposed the sensible thing to do under the present circumstances would be for us to get married. And I asked him if that was a proposal. And he said that he supposed it probably was.'

'How incredibly romantic!' Jonah observed.

'Yes, wasn't it?' Bernie agreed, with a grin. 'Anyway, one thing led to another and we got talking and in the end we fell asleep in each other's arms and the next thing we knew was Lucy, age five and a half, demanding to know what we were doing downstairs at that hour in the morning! And I'll never forget what she said after that. She said, "If you want to sleep together you'd be more comfy upstairs. Mam's bed is big enough for two people."'

I like to think that there was more to it than just a change to more convenient sleeping arrangements – although Bernie will persist in telling people that we only got married so that she wouldn't have to keep the sheets on the spare bed laundered! However, one thing that we never allowed ourselves to suppose was that Bernie could ever replace Angie – or I Richard.

I remember talking about that with Jonah. It was Angie's birthday and only a few months after Jonah's own wife, Margaret, died

'Bernie tells me you've got a Skype session with Eddie organised for tomorrow afternoon,' Jonah said, making conversation. 'Do you have something special to talk about?'

'It's Angie's birthday.'

'I'm sorry. I didn't know.'

'Of course not. Why should you?'

'Our Bernie keeps telling me I'm part of the family, so I feel I ought to know about that sort of thing.'

More silence.

'Peter?'

'Mmm?'

'If you don't mind me asking, how long does it take to really sink in? I mean how long was it before you kept expecting her to walk in the door any minute?'

'I'm sorry, I can't answer that. A long time – more than eleven years; that's all I can tell you.'

'Ah!' Jonah nodded. He knew full well that Angie had died a little over eleven years ago.

'But then, you wouldn't want to forget, would you?'

'No … I suppose we're the lucky ones, really. I mean, staying together till death us do part. We've never had someone walk out on us, like so many people these days.'

MIXED FEELINGS

(A painful period of my life in which my past tries to catch up with me.)

1 MIXED VOICES

When people hear that I was brought up in a children's home they often ask me whether I ever tried to find my 'real' parents. I can't really understand why they seem to think that I must be curious to know who it was who just happened to give birth to me, and the idea of actually trying to meet that person quite honestly never occurred to me.

Unfortunately, it turned out that the woman whose name is on my birth certificate had other ideas when, quite by chance, she happened upon me a full fifty-five years after having left me in the care of the National Children's Home. Bernie and I were still newly-weds, having got married five or six months previously. It was September 2006. Lucy, Bernie's daughter by her previous marriage, had just started in Year 2 – or the top class of the Infants in old money – and Bernie was away at a conference in Prague. There had been a spate of arson attacks on ethnic minority families, culminating in a house fire that killed three young children and their pregnant mother. I was leading the investigation and we decided to have a television appeal for witnesses, in the hope that someone would have seen something that would lead to us finding the perpetrators and preventing any more deaths and injuries.

If you read the accounts in the papers they say that I "made an impassioned plea" for people to come forward with information. Actually, all I did was to sit behind a desk and speak to camera, telling the viewers what had happened and asking them to think back over the past few weeks and try to remember if anyone they knew could have been involved. There was no need for any "impassioned pleading" on my part: I'm sure the public could all imagine what it must have been like for the father of the family coming home from his night shift and finding the house on fire with his wife and kids inside.

Anyway, we were pretty busy for a few days after that, with the lines jammed with people trying to get through to speak to members of the team. As usual, most of them didn't have anything particularly useful to say and a few were just attention-seekers, but we got quite a few worthwhile leads to follow up. However, that's another story.

The day after my TV appearance, we got a call from a Mrs Harris, who wouldn't say what she wanted except that she wouldn't speak to anyone except me personally. The constable who answered the phone tried to persuade her at least to tell her what sort of information she had to offer, but Mrs Harris just kept insisting that she wasn't prepared to divulge anything to anyone else. In the end, she passed the call on to me and I took it because we couldn't afford to risk missing out on any possible lead.

When I took the phone, I got the shock of my life. Instead of telling me anything pertinent to the investigation, the woman immediately started quizzing me about myself. She asked me if my date of birth was 16th March 1951 – which was spot on – and whether I'd grown up in a children's home. Of course, I refused to be drawn on either of these, but it was disconcerting that she seemed to know things about me that even my colleagues mostly did not. I kept pressing her politely either to provide us with information to help with our enquiries or to get off the line to allow other people to get through, but she just kept on asking me about myself – and I kept on refusing to answer.

Eventually she gave up trying to get me to admit to those details of my life – wherever she might have got them from. Presumably, she realised that I was never going to answer one way or the other and probably deduced that if I could have denied what she said, I would have done – so then she simply said that she was my mother and she wanted to arrange for us to meet.

I was so taken aback that it was as much as I could do

not to put the phone down on her without a word. However, I managed to say something reasonably polite – I'd got a room full of police officers listening in, after all, so I had to make a show of handling it professionally – before ringing off with the excuse that she evidently did not have anything to contribute and the line was needed for people who had.

Paul Godwin, who was my sergeant at the time and a good friend, asked what it was all about, but I just told him it was a nutter who just wanted to talk to me because she'd seen me on the telly. I was tempted to tell everyone to put the phone down on her right away, if she rang again, but I couldn't take the risk – however small it might be – that she did actually know something about the arsons.

I assumed that would be the end of the matter and tried to put it out of my mind, but it was strangely unsettling all the same. I was glad that the ongoing investigation kept me too busy to think about it. I was also glad that Bernie was back from her conference by the time the next development occurred a couple of weeks later.

2 Mixed Messages

A mysterious letter arrived in my office addressed to "Detective Inspector Peter Johns, Thames Valley Police, Oxford" and marked "Personal. FOR HIS EYES ONLY". It was dated just three days after the phone call from Mrs Harris, but it had taken quite some time to reach me, having been passed around internally for some time before anyone recognised my name.

Sergeant Godwin was there when I opened it and he gave me a bit of a funny look when he saw the photocopied birth certificate that was inside; but he understands when not to ask questions and didn't say anything. There was also a sheet of paper with scanned images of two photographs: a black and white one of a baby and a colour one of two women – one who looked to be in her sixties and a younger one – standing side by side. The covering letter was signed "your loving mother" and then in brackets "Mrs Valerie Harris". The address was Stockport, which was a relief, since it meant that she was, at least, too far off to make it easy for her to pop in for a visit.

As soon as I saw whom it was from, I stuffed the letter and its accompanying documents back in the envelope and put it away. My first instinct was to put the whole lot straight through the shredder, but then I decided to take it home to show Bernie first. I also toyed briefly with the idea of contacting Greater Manchester Police and asking them to warn the woman off – to tell her to stop bothering me – but I realised in time that I was overreacting. After all, it was only one letter and one phone call so far.

When Bernie saw the birth certificate, she immediately commented, 'well, she's got the date right anyhow.'

'It's not just the date,' I told her. I got out my own birth certificate – the one that I'd been given when I left the home – and showed her that the two were identical.

Mrs Harris had a copy of my birth certificate in her possession – not a photocopy of mine, but a second original certificate, like the ones you can buy when you register a baby's birth.

Bernie was more interested in my place of birth.

'Hoylake cum West Kirby!' she exclaimed. 'I never knew you came from across the water.'

'What do you mean?' I asked. 'What water?'

'The Mersey, of course. Anywhere on the Wirral is "across the water" from Liverpool. Didn't you know?'

'I never even knew that was where Hoylake cum West Kirby was,' I confessed. 'The names didn't mean a thing to me.'

Bernie picked up the photographs. There were handwritten notes underneath each of them, which indicated that they depicted "baby Peter, age 2 days" and "me with your sister, Jane".

'She doesn't have your red hair,' Bernie observed, 'but I suppose red hair often turns up in families unexpectedly – something to do with recessive genes. The birth certificate is interesting – don't you think it suggests she may be genuine?'

'It depends what you mean by that,' I said. 'She may well be the Valerie Johns on the certificate, but I don't see how that gives her the right to go round calling herself my mother. And I certainly don't see what right she has to persecute me like this!'

'What does she say she wants from you?'

'I don't know – I didn't read the letter properly,' I confessed, feeling a bit silly for not wanting to face up to it.

We read it together. Mrs Harris had "known at once" that I was her long-lost son as soon as she saw me, and heard my name, on the television. I was the "very image" of the older man who had fathered a child with her fifty-five years earlier. Her parents had insisted that she put the baby into a home and had refused to allow her to visit him.

Now that fate had thrown us together, she was eager to meet me and begged me to write back. She was now a widow, living with her daughter, Jane, in Stockport.

'It certainly all sounds plausible,' was Bernie's verdict. 'What are you going to do?'

'I don't see why I have to do anything!' I said, probably rather petulantly. The whole business had upset me more than I liked to admit. 'I just want her to go away and stop bothering me.'

'You're not even a bit curious to know what she's like?'

'No. she's just a complete stranger. She means nothing to me. All this "blood is thicker than water" business is a load of nonsense. It's the people you know – people like my houseparents and the other kids at the home and you and Angie and Hannah and Eddie and Lucy – that count.'

We sat for a while thinking.

'I can't decide,' I said at last. 'Do you think, if I ignore her, she'll get bored and stop hassling me? Or would it be better to write back and tell her to get lost?'

'I suppose the only sure-fire way to get her off your back would be to write back saying that isn't your birth certificate and you weren't brought up in a home and you already have some genuine parents, thank you very much!'

'But that would be dishonest.'

'Yes.'

'I'm very tempted.'

3 MIXED EMOTIONS

I really missed Angie over the next few weeks – even more than usual, I mean. I still could not make up my mind what to do about Mrs Harris, AKA my "mother", and I wished Angie were there to give me her opinion. I felt sure that she would have known what to do – and not been afraid to tell me.

Actually, I was pretty certain she would have said that I ought at least to meet the woman – if only to tell her face to face that I wanted no more to do with her. I rather fancy that was what Bernie thought too, but she was very careful not to give advice. She just kept saying that it was my choice and that nobody had a right to force me into anything I wasn't comfortable with.

I think it was because of that nagging feeling that Angie would have wanted me to give Mrs H a fair hearing that I did not simply destroy the letter and photos and everything right away. I stuffed them into a drawer while I dithered over whether or not I ought to ring the number in the letter and get it over with.

I suppose that must have gone on for two or three weeks before the decision was taken out of my hands by a new development.

4 MIXED COMPANY

'You have a visitor,' the desk sergeant said when I answered the phone in my office one day, about three weeks after I'd received the letter from my "mother". 'She says she's your sister.'

'I haven't got a sister,' I began. Then I remembered the photograph of two women with the caption "me with your sister, Jane" and realised, with a sinking feeling, that the visitor might well be this Jane. 'Never mind. I'll be right down.'

I went down to the reception area and found a short, dumpy woman who looked to be in her mid to late thirties. Her hair was a pale auburn, with a darker colour showing at the roots. She seemed to have a lot of makeup on her face: very shiny pink lipstick, something to make her cheeks red and rather garish (to my mind) green eyeshadow. Her eyebrows appeared to have been shaved off and then drawn on again in a high arch and her lashes were thick with mascara. I suppose she must have been trying to look her best for her new "brother".

She was wearing a full, floral-patterned skirt that came down below the tops of a pair of brown leather high-heeled boots, which I assume she thought made her look taller. In my opinion, they looked rather ridiculous.

When she saw me, she immediately got up and advanced towards me with her hands out. I managed to avoid the hug that she looked to be intending to bestow and shook her formally by the hand.

'Miss Jane Harris, I presume?'

'So you did get Mum's letter!' she exclaimed rather breathlessly. 'When you didn't write back, we thought it mustn't have found you. Yes, I'm Jane – but it's not Harris, it's Carrington. I changed my name when I got married and didn't bother to change back after the divorce.'

'And what can I do for you, Mrs Carrington?'

'Jane, please. After all, we are brother and sister, aren't we?'

'No,' I couldn't resist saying, 'I don't think we are.'

Her face fell.

'So, aren't you the right Peter Johns? Isn't that your birth certificate that Mum's been keeping all these years? Why didn't you say?'

'I'm not disputing that your mother may be the woman named on my birth certificate. I just don't accept that that gives her the right to go round calling herself my mother.'

'So who do you say is your mother, then?' she demanded, showing more spirit than she had up to then.

'No one. I don't have a mother. I never have had one. I managed without for fifty-five years and I don't intend to take one on now.'

I suppose that outburst must have sounded rather petulant, but I couldn't help myself. I just wanted to get rid of her and go back to life as normal. She sat looking at me for a moment without saying anything and I was just starting to hope that she would give up and go away, when she began again.

'Won't you at least come and meet her?' she pleaded. 'Mum has been ever so excited about the idea of finding you again. It will be awful for her if you reject her.'

'I'm not rejecting the bloody woman. She just irrelevant to me – don't you understand? Now, if you don't mind, I have a lot of work to do and can't afford to waste time chatting to you. Please, just go home and tell your mother to forget about whatever it was that happened to her fifty-odd years ago.'

But she wouldn't go. She just stood her ground and kept reiterating her demand that I meet with her mother, or if not meet in person, at least telephone or write. She got a photograph album out of her handbag and started trying to show me pictures of the Harris woman at different ages and various other members of what she insisted on calling "our family".

In the end, I noticed the desk sergeant watching us and I wondered how much of our conversation she had overheard. I decided there was nothing for it but to take Mrs Carrington away somewhere private, where we could talk more freely. I was still hoping that I could finally convince her to give up the idea that I was her long-lost brother, who was going to fall into her mother's arms and live happily ever after.

I put her in an interview room and then had the bright idea of calling Paul Godwin to join us. He came down right away, pleased to have an excuse to leave the paperwork that he had been doing. He has his own problems with his mother and father, so I knew I could trust him to have some sympathy with my predicament and not to blab about it afterwards.

'Sergeant,' I said when he entered the room, 'this is Mrs Jane Carrington. We are interviewing her on the subject of wasting police time and obstructing a police officer. Mrs Carrington, Sergeant Godwin is here to ensure that there is no dispute over what is said in this room. Do you understand?'

'No,' she said, looking around in confusion. 'I don't understand why you're taking this attitude. I would have thought you would have been pleased-'

'Sergeant,' I cut her off, 'do you remember a few weeks ago we got a call from a Mrs Harris purporting to be for the purpose of imparting information about the Cowley arson attacks?'

'I don't remember that call specifically,' Paul began, so I went on.

'She insisted on speaking to me personally. Do you remember the occasion now?'

'Yes, sir. I remember she kept you on the phone for some time and afterwards you said she had no information and was just wasting our time. You described her, as I recall, as "a nutter".'

'That's right, sergeant. Mrs Carrington is her daughter.

Now Mrs Carrington, tell me: were you aware of your mother's malicious telephone call to the team that was investigating several serious arson attacks?'

'She told me she'd rung, yes, but it wasn't malicious. She just didn't know how else to get to talk to you.'

'But while she was on the line, other members of the public couldn't get through. People with important information may have given up trying to give it to us as a result. She may have contributed to the fact that we still have not apprehended the offenders and that, since that time, two more attacks have taken place.'

I piled it on thick, hoping to shock her into giving up and advising her mother to do so as well.

'I never thought about it like that. And I'm sure Mum didn't either. She was just desperate to make contact with her son after all those years. Can't you understand that?'

'Did you encourage her to make the call?' I went on relentlessly, sensing that I had at last made some sort of impression on her.

'No. She didn't tell me about it until afterwards. We watched the news report together, and when she heard your name and saw your face, she said, "That's my Peter. He looks so like his father! It must be my Peter!" Then she went very quiet and thoughtful. She rang you the next day while I was at work and I only knew about it when she told me that you wouldn't answer her questions and she didn't know what to do next.'

'I see. So you weren't an accomplice in the offence, but you are confirming that your mother, Mrs Harris, deliberately rang a police hotline although she did not have any information for the enquiry?'

'But she didn't mean to interfere with the investigation. She never thought about her call preventing other people getting through. Anyway – you ought to have more lines, if one person can make a difference like that. You can't be serious. You're not really thinking of charging her, are you?'

I have to admit that, for a moment or two, I was tempted to string her along for a bit longer. Maybe it was because I couldn't trust myself to behave reasonably that I'd called Paul Godwin in.

'No,' I said in the end. 'We won't be charging her – or you – just so long as you go away quietly now and stop preventing me from getting on with my work.'

She got up as if to go and then seemed to change her mind and sat down again. She looked me in the eye and said very coldly, 'I think you are being very callous. Our mother believes that the reason you didn't reply to her letter is because you blame her for deserting you all those years ago. Why can't you at least have the decency to tell her that you forgive her?'

For a moment, I couldn't think what to say. I started to feel guilty for not having replied, but then I felt angry that she was using moral blackmail to get me to do something that I was convinced would be a big mistake for all of us.

'Well,' I said in the end, 'tell her from me that there's nothing to forgive. I had a happy, stable childhood and a wonderful marriage, and I've got a good job that I enjoy and some wonderful kids and everything is just fine. She has absolutely nothing to reproach herself about at all.'

'If all that's true,' she argued, 'why can't you tell her yourself? What are you frightened of?'

That really struck home, because, of course, she'd hit the nail on the head. I *was* frightened of meeting my "mother" – I will always think of the word in inverted commas – and being expected to form some sort of relationship with this stranger. I suppose that's why I found myself saying things that afterwards I realised were rather cruel. 'I'm not frightened,' I lied. 'I just know that all this bringing long lost relatives back together business is a load of nonsense. We can't possibly have anything in common, so meeting up is bound to mean disappointment all round. Tell your mother that she did the right thing putting me into the care of the NCH. I'm sure I was much better off than I would have been with her in whatever circumstances she was in then. I've never had a mother and I'm too old to start now. I don't need a mother – or a sister for that matter. I've got all the family I need already. So now, Sergeant Godwin is going to escort you out and I will leave instructions with the front desk that you are not to be allowed in again. Do you understand?'

5 MIXED REVIEWS

As I said before, I've never been able to understand why people who were adopted or fostered would have a desire to trace their birth parents. I would far rather let sleeping dogs lie.

I suppose, from a purely practical point of view, there might be some benefit in knowing if you have a family history of various illnesses – my doctor certainly seems to think that I'm disadvantaged by never being able to answer his questions on the subject – but I'm sceptical even of that. What's the good of knowing that you have a higher than average chance of developing some unpleasant disease? I know I'd rather be in ignorance than being like Bernie, living with the knowledge that she's already reached a greater age than either of her parents did. And always having at the back of her mind the possibility that she might have inherited a predisposition to motor neurone disease from her mother. Not to mention hoping against hope that she'll manage to survive long enough to see Lucy through university. She never talks about it, but I know she worries.

But I digress.

I told Bernie about Jane Carrington's visit. We were sitting in the kitchen having "a brew" after putting Lucy to bed. Bernie didn't say much, but I could see from her face that she was anxious about the effect that the letter and now this meeting was having on me. When I started telling her about what Jane had said about her mother wanting me to tell her I forgave her, she put out her hand and took hold of mine. I think she wanted to be supportive, but couldn't honestly say that she thought I'd got things right.

Round about that point in the conversation, Stan came in from the garden to wash his hands at the sink. He had been feeding his pigeons. Afterwards, he dried his hands very slowly and deliberately, and then came over and sat down with us.

'I know it's none of my business,' he began, 'but I couldn't help overhearing.'

Neither Bernie nor I said anything, so he went on.

'I have to say, young Peter, that I thought better of you.'

'What do you mean?' Bernie asked sharply, giving him a hard look. 'I'm sure she knew what he was getting at, but she didn't like anyone criticising me – especially when she knew how badly I was feeling.'

'I mean – I always had you down as a kind sort of person, but what you said to that poor woman wasn't kind at all, was it?'

I stared down at the table, feeling like a small boy who had been told off by a favourite teacher.

'Have you tried to see it from your mother's point of view?' he asked, remorselessly. 'How do you know that she didn't want desperately to keep her baby, but other people prevented her? How do you know that she hasn't been longing all these years to find him? And now she does, and all you can say is, "I'm glad you gave me away because you'd have been a rotten mother anyway!"'

'Peter never said that!' Bernie protested.

'As good as – eh, Peter?'

'Yes,' I admitted. 'I knew I was out of order a soon as I'd said it, but it was too late then. I just wanted to make them go away!'

'Well, it's your choice,' Stan said, getting up to go. 'I'd just like to suggest that it wouldn't really do you so much harm just to pick up the phone and speak to her yourself.'

Of course, I knew he was right. I had known all along that I couldn't leave things the way they were. But it was a long time before I could pluck up the courage to ring the number that my "mother" had given in her letter. What could we possibly have to say to one another? How could I prevent her developing expectations that we would continue to communicate and ultimately to forge some sort of "relationship" with one another, without saying things that would be hurtful to her?

When I did eventually ring, she was pathetically grateful to me. However many times I reiterated that no blame attached to her, she seemed unable to comprehend that I did not hold it against her that she had abandoned me – as she saw it – as a baby. She kept thanking me for be prepared to speak to her despite what she had put me through – and was quite impervious to my protestations that she hadn't put me through anything at all!

In the end, the only way I managed to get her off the line was to agree that we would meet – just once – so that she could see for herself how I had turned out and whether I looked as much like my "father" as she remembered I had done from the TV appearance. The whole idea was very much against my better judgement, but, remembering how disappointed Stan had been in me, I didn't dare to express my dislike of the idea as forcefully as I would have liked to have done. I did put my foot down at her suggestion that I might come to stay at her house. I insisted that we meet on neutral territory.

In the end, we agreed on Manchester Piccadilly Station, which was as convenient as anywhere and would provide both parties with an easy exit if things went wrong. She tried to persuade me to bring the kids with me, but I refused. I had no intention of ever letting on about her existence to either Hannah or Eddie.

6 MIXED DOUBLES

We left Lucy with Sylvia and Stan for the day and Bernie and I went up to Manchester on the train. I didn't want to face the Harris woman and her daughter alone!

Bernie, for whom the journey as far as Crewe was very familiar, chatted cheerfully and pointed out landmarks on the way, trying to keep my spirits up. Not particularly successfully, I have to say. I was becoming increasingly convinced that it had been a mistake to allow myself to be talked into this meeting. We alighted at Piccadilly, and Bernie commented on how new and clean the station looked now, following the renovations that had been done for the Commonwealth Games a few years earlier.

We walked hand-in-hand along the platform. As soon as we got out on to the concourse, there they were! Valerie Harris was slightly taller than her daughter. She had black hair, which I assumed was dyed, and brown eyes. She looked much younger than I had expected. When she saw us, she stepped forward with her arms outstretched. Bernie and I held hands tightly and I pulled her a bit closer to me in case my "mother" had any fancy ideas of attempting to hug me.

I think that probably was what she had in mind initially, but she took the hint and both women shook hands quite sensibly when I held mine out to them. I introduced Bernie and we all made our way to a coffee shop where we could talk.

I'll leave Valerie's story to another chapter, so that I can include various things that I only heard about later. So when you read this account of our conversation you need to remember that I'm missing out all the things she told me about how I came to be conceived and who my "father" was and what her parents said and did when they discovered she was pregnant.

The first hurdle to overcome was how we would address one another. She wanted me to call her "mum" but I wasn't having any of that. I suggested "Mrs Harris" but she was so clearly upset by the idea that I gave way and we compromised on first names all round.

After that, I think Valerie got the message that I wasn't particularly keen on furthering our relationship and she turned her attention to Bernie. Perhaps she thought that, being a woman, Bernie would be more interested in family ties.

'What do you do, dear?' Valerie asked, 'now that the children have left home.'

I'd told her on the phone that I had two kids and I'd told her their ages, but not their names or where they lived. She was a bit put out about that. She had evidently had hopes of corresponding with her grandchildren, but I was not going to give her a chance to disrupt their lives the way she had mine.

'I teach maths at St Luke's,' Bernie told her. This is her stock answer when she wants to play down her status. When she says this, most people outside academic circles assume that St Luke's is a school or at most a Further Education college.

'That's nice. Jane's a teacher, aren't you?' she said, turning to her daughter.

'Yes,' Jane agreed. 'Primary – early years.'

'And what about your daughter?' Valerie asked, still trying to make conversation with Bernie. 'Is she following in your footsteps?'

'Since she's only six,' Bernie answered,' she hasn't made up her mind about a career yet.'

'I'm sorry,' Valerie turned to me with a puzzled expression, 'I was sure you said your daughter was in her twenties.'

'That's right,' I agreed, getting guilty pleasure from her confusion.

Bernie took pity on her and explained that I'd been married before and that, therefore, my children weren't her children.

'So now you've got a new young family,' Valerie commented. 'Rather like me. I had you and then it was twenty years before I had Jane. How do your older children like having a little sister?'

'It's not really like that,' Bernie explained, with commendable patience. 'They both knew her before Peter and I were married – from birth in fact – so it really hasn't made a great deal of difference to them.'

'It isn't as if they were still living with me,' I pointed out.

'So having a wicked stepmother hasn't really affected them at all,' Bernie added.

Eventually we got our family relationships sorted out in Valerie's mind. For some reason she got ridiculously excited at the idea that Bernie and I were newlyweds and was very disappointed when Bernie couldn't show her any pictures of the wedding and was unable to describe the dresses beyond saying that the bridesmaids had worn 'long blue lacy things'. We didn't bother to mention that Bernie hadn't worn a dress at all, preferring to come in black trousers. In retrospect, perhaps it would have been a good idea to impress upon Valerie more of our eccentricities in the hope that she might have been put off by them.

Valerie insisted on showing us a tatty black and white photograph of a man who looked to be in his forties, whom she described as "your father". She held it out to Bernie with the words, 'Don't you agree that Peter is the very image of his father?'

Bernie looked at the picture politely and said something non-committal. Afterwards, on the train home, she confessed to me that she thought there was a strong family resemblance and it was not at all surprising that Valerie had recognised it when she saw me at the press conference. I suppose I do know now where I got my red hair!

'I would have sent you a copy,' Valerie explained, 'but, as you can see, it's not in very good condition and the photocopy just didn't do him justice. I had to keep it hidden away, you see – in case my parents found it.'

She was very disappointed that I hadn't brought any pictures of my kids, but I was determined not to give her any possible means of tracing them and making contact. Leeds, where Hannah lives, is far too close to Stockport for comfort and I know that Hannah often goes shopping in Manchester, so it wouldn't be impossible that they might happen to bump into one another. She then asked about what they were doing and where they lived. I told her that my daughter was a nurse, like her mother, and my son was in computers, but I refused to give any hints as to their location.

Jane was being rather left out of the conversation, so Bernie tried to divert attention away from the inquisition that Valerie was subjecting me to by asking her about her own family.

'I can't have children,' Jane said. 'At least – my ex-husband has had three with his new wife, so I assume that it was my fault that we didn't have any.'

'It's such a pity, isn't it?' Valerie chipped in. 'I was beginning to think I would never be a grandmother, which is another reason why it's so wonderful to have found you again, Peter.'

Bernie and I looked at each other, but neither of us could think of anything to say to that. It was clear that Valerie was hoping that I would fill what she obviously thought of as a serious gap in her life caused by her only daughter having let her down in respect of producing grandchildren for her. That realisation made the whole sorry situation even worse – if that were possible.

We struggled on for an hour or so longer. Valerie made all the running in the conversation. Bernie and I tried to remember to nod and smile at appropriate points and Jane answered whenever her mother turned to her for confirmation of something that she had said. Eventually I decided that enough was enough and I got up, saying that we had better be getting back to Lucy.

Valerie pressed me to give her a phone number or address, but I wasn't prepared to give her a way of approaching me again. I tried to impress on her that this was a one-off meeting and she ought to try to forget all about me. Of course, she didn't accept that and I did feel rather bad about leaving her like that, because she did seem genuinely upset.

I asked Bernie on the way home whether she thought I was being unfair. She thought for a bit and then said that she supposed that at least now perhaps Valerie might start valuing Jane a bit more, seeing as her other offspring had turned out to be so unsatisfactory! I wasn't sure how to take that, but I think she's right that Jane is the one who has really lost out in all this. It must be dreadful for her to find herself being pushed out in favour of some long lost brother turning up out of the blue with a wife and kids and a successful career, when she's lived with her mother all these years and is now seen by her as a failure.

7 MIXED FORTUNES

I said that I would tell you Valerie's story, so here goes! I suppose in some ways it's very much the sort of thing I'd expected it to be.

Valerie Johns lived with her parents in Croxteth, which is a suburb of Liverpool. I could see Bernie's ears pricking up when Valerie told us where she had come from, but she refrained from saying anything – which was unusual for her. She's normally delighted to have an excuse to talk about her native city, but she knew I didn't want to do anything to encourage Valerie to think that we were going to form a long-term friendship or had anything whatever in common.

When she was twelve, Valerie started learning to play the piano, under the tuition of a Mr Lewis. She used to call at his house after school for her lessons. He was in his late thirties and unmarried. They got on very well together and after a few months, it wasn't just piano-playing that he was teaching her. She was still only thirteen when she fell pregnant.

This was all way before the Abortion Act – and in any case, she was so young and inexperienced that it was too late by the time she realised what was happening to her – so she had no choice but to have the baby. Her parents were horrified when they found out and they packed her off to stay with an aunt in Hoylake in an attempt to avoid a scandal. Valerie stayed there until after the birth. Meanwhile, her parents decided to up sticks and move the whole family down the East Lancashire Road to Manchester, where no one would know them and there would be no awkward questions asked about their wayward daughter.

Lewis appears to have got away scot-free. When I asked Valerie whether they had reported him to the police, she seemed quite taken aback, as if she had never thought about the fact that he had committed an offence. I suppose she was too young to understand such things and her parents were afraid of drawing attention to something that they clearly saw as shameful.

Valerie pleaded to be allowed to keep her baby, but she was overruled by her family and forced to hand me over to the care of the National Children's Home. She said that she always intended to go back and claim me when she was old enough, and she was full of remorse that she never did.

She claimed that she was in love with Peter Lewis – although exactly what sort of love a thirteen-year-old child might have for a mature man is questionable – and that he loved her. Most likely, she felt she owed it to herself – or to me – to have been in love with the father of her child. Although, I suppose her choice of name for me must be of some significance.

Anyway, that's how things were. Valerie's parents arranged for me to be placed in a home well away from where they were living, to make it more difficult for her to attempt to visit. They wanted me to be put up for adoption – which they saw as a way of drawing a line under the unfortunate incident once and for all – but Valerie held out against that, with surprising strength of will under the circumstances. She kept telling me that she worried that this might have been wrong, because if she hadn't clung on to the idea that she would reclaim me eventually, I might have had a normal family life. I hope I managed to convince her that no damage was done and my childhood was every bit as happy as the majority of families.

Valerie finished school and started work in a department store. Her parents kept her on a very short rein so she didn't get to meet many people of her own age socially, but a young man from the menswear department took a fancy to her and asked her out. A few months later, he asked her to marry him. Seeing a way of getting out from under her parents' control and establishing a home of her own, she accepted and they moved into a house in Wythenshawe.

To her parents' horror, Valerie was completely open with Jack Harris about her previous liaison and her desire to look after her child – now seven years old – herself. Jack, who probably comes out of all this better than anyone else, was willing to go along with the idea.

However, before they could act they were overtaken by events. Valerie found herself pregnant again and it looked as if they would have their own family to worry about. They agreed to put off finding and claiming her first born until the new baby was settled.

Valerie suffered a miscarriage, which put her into a state of depression for quite some time. The verdict of the doctors was that her having previously given birth at such a young age had caused some permanent damage and it was unlikely that she would ever carry another child to full term. Valerie was distraught at the idea that she might not have any more children.

After five more miscarriages, she finally gave birth to Jane.

'But afterwards,' she told us tearfully, 'I had everything taken away. They said it would be too dangerous for me to try for any more children.'

By now, the idea of adopting Valerie's first baby was almost forgotten, in the emotional upheaval of the repeated hopes and disappointments and the final blow to her hopes of a large family. Additionally, she realised that her "baby" was by now a young man, who could even have embarked on setting up his own home and starting a family. (Indeed, my "sister" Jane is closer in age to my kids than to me.) So, fortunately, Valerie and Jack decided not to attempt to track me down after all.

Jane was the apple of her parents' eye – unsurprisingly after the trouble they had bringing her into the world. They were proud when she went to college and trained as a teacher, and delighted when she married a fellow-teacher,

Brendan Carrington. Valerie started looking forward eagerly for the arrival of grandchildren.

According to Jane, Brendan was also keen for the patter of tiny feet; but after six years, it began to look as if this was not going to happen. Brendan started to look elsewhere.

'I suppose men always need to prove themselves,' Jane told us. 'He needed to demonstrate to himself that he was capable of fathering a child. And then, of course, once he'd got Daphne pregnant, it was inevitable that he'd leave me and go off with her.' The whole business makes a very sad story and I can't help feeling sorry for both Valerie and Jane. I just wish Valerie hadn't been relying on me to restore her status with the Women's Institute and the Knitting Club by enabling her to compete in the grandmother stakes! I suppose that her frustration at there being no likelihood of any grandchildren, coupled with her husband's death at the age of sixty-eight, made it inevitable that she should start thinking again of the baby that she'd given up fifty-odd years previously. It's no wonder she saw it as some sort of miracle when she heard my name on the television and managed to convince herself that I looked like the man who had fathered that child all those years ago.

8 MIXED NUMBERS

After the meeting in Manchester I hoped that would be the end of the matter and we could get back to our lives and forget about Valerie and her unfortunate daughter, Jane. But I was not taking into account the tenacity of a mother deprived of her child – which I assume must be how Valerie saw the situation.

I'd been careful not to give her any way of contacting me direct. Our home phone line was ex-directory – and in any case would not have been under my name. I had not divulged our address and I'd left strict instructions to my colleagues not to accept any communications from Valerie or Jane through the police. What I hadn't thought of was how easy it is to obtain email addresses and direct line telephone numbers for academics, who routinely put such information on their university web pages.

It wasn't long before Bernie started receiving emails and telephone calls from Valerie, begging her to facilitate another meeting and sending messages for me. At first, Bernie dutifully passed the messages on; but, when she saw how upset they made me, she soon stopped and I assumed that the calls and emails must have stopped too.

Bernie dealt with the emails easily by setting up her emailer to consign anything coming from Valerie to the Spam folder; but, as she only told me much later, the daily (sometimes more) telephone calls became something of a nuisance. Eventually she arranged with her college to be given a new number, which she carefully avoided publicising.

I can't make up my mind whether I'm glad or sorry that Bernie didn't tell me about all this at the time. I feel bad that she was having to put up with such harassment on my behalf, but if I'd known I might have decided to take things further – getting a court injunction against Valerie or something – which would probably have only caused a lot of trouble and heartache all round.

9 MIXED GENERATIONS

About eighteen months after Valerie first attempted to contact me – and more than a year after our meeting – things suddenly took an unexpected turn. Bernie received a call from the Porters' Lodge at her college saying that a Mrs Jane Carrington was anxious to see her. Her first instinct was to ask the porter to send her away, but there was something about the way the porter spoke that made her think that she had better go over and speak to Jane herself.

To cut a long story short, Jane told Bernie that her mother had been diagnosed with cancer and was only expected to live for a matter of a few months at most. She was distraught at the idea that she might die without ever having even seen what her grandchildren looked like and had begged Jane to find Peter and to persuade him to come to see her again and to bring his children.

Bernie knew that nothing in the world would ever persuade me to involve Hannah or Eddie, and she was very reluctant even to suggest to me that I might go to see Valerie. She urged Jane to go back to her mother and tell her to forget all about me, but Jane had come on a mission and wasn't prepared to go away empty-handed. So Bernie promised that she would speak to me and that one or other of us would ring Jane to tell her what we had decided. Well, of course, under the circumstances, I could hardly continue to refuse to see her, could I? So, very much against my better judgement, we agreed to go up to Stockport and see Valerie in her home; and I promised to bring photographs of "the grandchildren".

10 MIXED MARRIAGE

If this were one of those television reunion programmes, Valerie and I would have fallen on one another's necks weeping and then spent the remainder of her life in some sort of bittersweet love-in. If it were fiction, the author might even throw in a miraculous recovery so that we could live happily ever afterwards until Valerie finally passed away peacefully at a grand old age. But this is real life and it turned out quite differently.

We drove up to Stockport, having decided that would make getting away at a moment's notice easier than if we were tied to railway timetables. Valerie and Jane lived in a pleasant nineteen-thirties semi-detached house on the outskirts of the town. We parked outside and walked slowly up the path to the front door, which was opened immediately by Jane, who must have been watching out for us.

She led us inside and showed us into a bright sunny room at the back of the house, where Valerie was reclining on a sofa. She looked very pale and seemed to have lost weight. She held her hands wide in a gesture presumably intended to invite me to embrace her, but I shook her hand formally and said something bland about being sorry to hear that she was ill.

With the idea of getting things over with as quickly as possible, I took out the photographs that I had brought. I'd chosen Hannah's and Eddie's graduation pictures. Not the close-up ones, which might have allowed Valerie or Jane to recognise them in the street, but the full-length ones showing them standing in gown and mortar-board holding their degree certificate tied up with red ribbon. Hannah's had Angie and me standing on either side of her. I handed it to Valerie.

'This is my eldest,' I said. 'She was the first person in the family to get a degree. We were very proud of her.'

Valerie took the photograph with a smile and looked

down, evidently expecting to share in our pride. Then her face suddenly changed and I'm sure she shuddered and recoiled in disgust. She looked round at Bernie and me in bewilderment with what I can only describe as a look of horror on her face.

'This can't be right,' she said at last. 'This isn't my granddaughter. It can't be!'

I'd often seen people being taken aback by finding that my kids have dark brown skin and afro-type hair, but this was the first time that I'd seen such revulsion as Valerie displayed. My immediate impulse was to shout at her that of course Hannah was her grandchild and she'd better get used to the idea of having a couple of black kids in her family. At least, that was my impulse after I'd restrained myself from simply hitting her in the face and storming out. But then I thought of an even better way of making her pay for her abhorrent reaction.

'No,' I agreed, speaking as calmly as I could, 'this is not your granddaughter, because I am not your son. We are complete strangers with nothing in common. The fact that your name happens to be on my birth certificate is a complete irrelevancy. I'm glad you understand that at last.'

I got up, planning to make a dignified exit before I was tempted to say any more, but Valerie clutched at my sleeve and pulled me back.

'This other black woman,' she said, pointing at the photograph. 'That's your first wife, I suppose?'

'Yes. Do you have a problem with that?'

'Why did you have to marry a black?' she asked, looking up at me with a mixture of puzzlement and anxiety. 'Was it because you'd been in a home?'

'What a ridiculous question! I can't think what you mean.' I tried to pull away, but she held on with a surprisingly firm grip.

'I mean – did the other girls think you weren't good enough, because you didn't have a proper family?'

I jerked my arm away and stood looking down at her. For several seconds I could not think of anything to say to this preposterous remark.

'I married Angie because we were in love,' I said at last. 'I never regretted it for a single moment of the twenty-five years that we were together – right up to the day that some other bigoted lunatic, like you, stabbed her to death in her own kitchen for being different from them. And now, I think we'd better be going. I'm sure you won't want to have someone like me in your house for any longer than you have to.'

I was hoping to get away without actually coming to blows or having a shouting match, but I hadn't reckoned with Valerie's outstanding talent for making crass remarks.

'But surely,' she said, 'you would have preferred to marry a nice English girl – like your present wife, for instance.'

Up until now, Bernie had been uncharacteristically silent, believing that this business was just between Valerie and me. But now, having in effect been appealed to as a witness to support Valerie's side of the argument, she let rip, her accent becoming more and more broad Scouse as she got into her stride.

'Now look here, you,' she began. 'You've no right to speak like that about someone you haven't even met. Peter's wife was the best friend I ever had and if you think you can say differently, you're talking through your hat. How dare you judge her based on the colour of her skin! And how dare you persecute Peter the way you have? Can't you see what you've been doing to him, stalking him like that? It's about time you started taking some notice of your daughter, who's been sticking by you all these years, with precious little thanks as far as I can tell, instead of chasing after the son that you imagine you ought to have but which you don't deserve and who is worth ten of you. You're just a prejudiced old cow who thinks the world owes her, just because she's dying. Well, my mother died when she was forty, having never had a bad word to say about anyone, and Peter's wife was killed before she reached fifty because of people like you. So don't imagine that you deserve our sympathy when you can't even appreciate what a sacrifice it was for Peter to bring you those photos, after he'd promised himself he wasn't going to let you get your claws into his kids the way you have with him.'

She paused for breath and I took the opportunity to make our exit.

'Thank you for your hospitality, Mrs Harrison,' I said, speaking very formally and avoiding eye contact with our host. 'Now we really must be going. It's a long drive back to Oxford.'

Jane showed us to the door. I fancied that there was a hint of relief on her face and wondered if she was grateful to Bernie for having drawn her mother's attention to the way in which she had been pushed into second-place by the arrival of her estranged half-brother.

We got into the car and drove off. After a few minutes, Bernie spoke in a rather small voice.

'I'm sorry Peter. I was out of order saying all those things. It's just that she did make me so angry.'

'You only said the things I would like to have said but didn't have the courage.'

'But she is elderly and dying and probably only has the attitudes that she was brought up with.'

'That's what really worries me,' I admitted. 'I can't get it out of my head that I might think like that if she'd decided to keep her baby instead of putting me in the home.'

'Oh Peter!' Bernie put her arm round my shoulders and then withdrew it when she realised that it was impeding my ability to drive. 'I can't imagine you holding those ridiculous views, but I do see what you mean. It's a horrible thought, isn't it?'

11 MIXED ECONOMY

That's about all, really. Bernie and I went home and we both tried to forget all about Valerie and Jane. They, in their turn, did not attempt to get in touch with us again. That is, until, a few months later, a card arrived at Bernie's college, simply informing us that Valerie had died and giving the time and venue of the funeral. Needless to say, we did not attend.

Then, the following week, a solicitor called the police station wanting to speak to me. It turned out that Valerie had made a new will – after our first meeting in Manchester and before the final one in Stockport – making me her executor and joint residual legatee with Jane, the estate being equally divided between us. It seemed, from what the solicitor said that Valerie did not consider the role of executor to be appropriate for a woman. (You can imagine what Bernie said about that when I told her!) That, apparently, was one reason why she had been so pleased to have found her long-lost son.

Naturally, I wasn't prepared to accept her money. That would have been the case even if I had been her only surviving relative but, as things stood, it was clearly impossible for me to take my share because it would have forced Jane to sell up the family home where she was living.

Jane was ridiculously grateful when I refused to act as executor, renounced the inheritance and handed it all over to her. I don't like to think that she thought I was hypocritical enough to have taken her mother's property after everything that I (and Bernie) had said; but, I suppose a lot of people do change their attitudes when there's money at stake. As far as I'm concerned, she's welcome to my thirty pieces of silver as well as her own share. She's earned it, living with Valerie all those years and putting up with her moaning about how she wasn't able to provide her with any grandchildren and, no doubt, indoctrinating her with all sorts of bigoted ideas.

Jane did suggest that we might correspond occasionally. I suppose she thought she ought to make some sort of gesture to show her appreciation of what she clearly viewed as my Grand Gesture. I declined politely. I think Bernie was probably a bit more direct in her response to Jane's final email correspondence. Anyway, the message finally got through and we haven't heard from her since. I cannot tell you what a relief it is to know that I can get on with my life without worrying that some long-lost relative might suddenly turn up on the doorstep. And I am infinitely glad that neither Hannah nor Eddie ever found out about the existence of their so-called grandmother.

SIBLING RIVALRY

(My attempt to answer the oft-repeated question: but *why* do you have Jonah living with you in your house?)

1 INTRODUCTION

People often ask me if I resent allowing another man to come into my family and take up so much of my wife's time. It's a funny thing because that wasn't how it happened at all. However, there have been times when seeing more of Jonah Porter would have been the very last thing I would have hoped for. When we worked together under DCI Richard Paige, I often felt that I was given all the routine stuff to do while Jonah was allowed to indulge himself with investigating his own, sometimes rather fanciful, ideas. It didn't make it any better that those ideas so often seemed to turn out to be right!

I think that probably the people who knew us both at that time are the ones who find it most strange that Bernie and I have welcomed him into our house as a permanent part of the family. I've actually heard some of them suggesting that it's unfair of Bernie to be inflicting him on me – which isn't what it's like at all. And others seem to think that I'm some sort of saint or hero to put up with him – which is nonsense as well.

So, here's my attempt at setting the record straight. I hope that by the end of it you'll have realised that none of us – least of all me – is as heroic or unselfish as some people would have you believe. I'm also hoping that you'll get to understand that, contrary to outward appearances, I do have a say in what goes on in my own house and nobody has been inflicting anything on me at all!

2. LET'S START AT THE VERY BEGINNING

I first made the acquaintance of PC Jonah Porter back in November 1979. I'd been a Detective Sergeant for about eighteen months and married to Angie for a month or so less than that. It was a Sunday morning and Angie was getting ready to go to church when the phone rang summoning me to attend a suspicious death in a multi-occupancy house in North Oxford. If you've ever lived in a university town, you'll know the sort of thing I mean: a big Victorian semi-detached divided into rooms for students or young professionals with a communal kitchen and bathroom.

Richard picked me up from home in his car and we went together to the house. By the time we got there, an ambulance was already pulled up outside and the front door was open. We rang the bell to announce our arrival, but we didn't wait to be invited before we went on in. There was a very young-looking constable standing there in the hall speaking to a young woman whose face looked vaguely familiar, but which I couldn't place. I worked out afterwards that I'd probably seen her at the hospital on some occasion when I'd dropped Angie off there for work or when we were investigating an assault and had to go to A&E with the victim. She turned out to be Dr Margaret Hulme, a Junior Doctor training to be a trauma surgeon. The constable was, of course, Jonah.

He showed us through to one of the bed-sits where a quite bizarre scene greeted us. There was the dead body of a young man lying naked in bed surrounded by a collection of apparently random objects. I don't have my notes to hand, but I remember there being a pair of union jack underpants, a couple of mugs, a photograph in a frame, a fountain pen – and a cuddly toy! It sounds like the conveyor belt on an episode of the *Generation Game*, doesn't it? We were standing there puzzling over what on earth they were there for, when Jonah piped up to say that he knows what they all are.

That's the point at which Richard really starts taking notice of the young copper. It turns out that Jonah has been seeing the attractive young doctor, Margaret, and that they've been doing a bit if detective work themselves, in connection with some petty thieving that has been going on in the house. All the objects lying on the bed around the murder victim are items that belong to residents of the house. And they've all been stolen in the last few months.

Anyway, the upshot of all that was that Richard went upstairs to Margaret's room to see what they'd found out about the thefts, while I was left keeping order among the other residents, who were all in the communal living room waiting to be interviewed.

After a few minutes, Jonah put his head round the door and called me out. He told me that DI Paige wanted everyone to be sent back to wait in their rooms so that he could interview them each individually in the living room. I organised that, and then we talked to each of the housemates in turn. Richard allowed Jonah to sit in on all the interviews, although, as I discovered later, he wasn't even supposed to be in North Oxford that day. He was only there because Margaret had called him personally, after dialling 999. I remember Richard having quite a lot of explaining to do to the officer who had assigned Jonah to patrol the troublesome Blackbird Leys Estate that morning! If Richard hadn't been so senior – and so well-liked and respected within the force – Jonah might have been in trouble about that.

Richard made a bit of a speciality of spotting promising young uniformed officers and recruiting them into CID. He did that with me and I could see, from the moment Jonah confessed to his amateur investigation with Margaret, that Richard was sizing him up as another potential protégé. It was also obvious to me from early on that Richard had his eye on Jonah's relationship with Margaret and was going to do anything he could to nudge it along.

He had a very romantic streak, had Richard, and he always hoped to be able to produce a happy ending when he saw young people falling for one another. I never could work out how it was that he never so much as asked a girl out himself. Well, actually, at the time I thought I'd sussed it, because I'd spotted a woman's photograph in his wallet and I'd guessed that it was some old sweetheart from this youth that he'd never been able to forget. It turned out that I was wrong about that. It was actually his mother! She'd run off when he was only a kid and he'd treasured this old photo ever since. Bernie's theory – which is probably right – is that he was so traumatised by that, and by thinking that it must have been his fault that she left, that he could never believe that anyone would care for him.

But I digress. This chapter was supposed to be about my first encounter with Jonah. So, where was I? That's right! Jonah's investigation into the petty thefts turned out to be crucial to discovering who had killed the student, Simon Coulter. This has all been dealt with elsewhere, so I won't go into the details. The significant thing was that this Simon was a nasty piece of work who had victimised some of the others in a very nasty way. I particularly remember one of the other students – a postgraduate from Germany – describing him as *creepy*. I can hear his words now, as I think back.

'Like most postgraduates, he gave tutorials to undergraduates,' he told us. 'Last summer, just after taking his final examinations, one of these students jumped to his death from the top of the engineering building. Speaking about it afterwards, Simon did not appear at all concerned about the death of this young man. In fact, he said to me that he had told the student in question that he might as well give up the idea of doing a DPhil because he had no chance of getting a first class degree. I got the impression that he was rather pleased – proud even – to think that he might have contributed towards making the young man take his own life.'

It was only years and years afterwards, when Jonah and I compared notes, that I twigged that the student that jumped from the engineering tower was Bernie's fiancé, Stephen. It's a small world, as they say!

The other thing that sticks in my mind from that investigation is the way that Jonah allowed his single-minded pursuit of the culprit to lead him into making what was almost an accusation against Margaret. I could see it amused Richard no end to see him following a train of thought that inevitably led to the conclusion that she was a very likely suspect indeed. I can see him now, with a sort of half-smile on his face saying, 'Well now, Porter, as I said, I'm impressed. You're thinking like a detective. But a word of advice: unless you have ambitions to end up as an old bachelor like me, possibly you ought to be a bit more circumspect about accusing your girlfriends of murder to their faces. In my experience a lot of women take offence that that sort of thing.'

Margaret immediately backed Jonah up, which was exactly the right thing to do to get Richard well and truly on her side and rooting for them to get it together. It was no surprise to me when he invited Jonah back with us to talk through the case and plan our next move. And I was pretty certain by then that the next move, after the case was wrapped up, would be an application for Constable Porter to be transferred to Richard's team in CID.

3. THREE'S A CROWD

I joined CID at more or less the same time as Richard got his promotion to Detective Inspector. For some reason he chose me as his 'bag carrier' to accompany him when he went out to investigate cases. I suppose that maybe he was afraid that he might find it difficult to impose his authority on a Detective Sergeant when he'd only just moved up from that rank himself. Anyway, it was excellent training for me in the art of detection and in particular in dealing sensitively with victims of crime and in interviewing witnesses without antagonising them.

Richard pushed me to take my sergeant's exams and I think he also used his influence to get me promoted. I owe him an awful lot – not least, because I doubt if I would have felt able to propose marriage to Angie if I hadn't had the extra security of a sergeant's pay to offer her. That made the difference between being stuck in police accommodation for the foreseeable future and being able to get a mortgage on a small house in East Oxford.

When Jonah joined the team, I found that increasingly we were going round in a threesome. In theory, I was showing Jonah the ropes – and to be fair to Richard, he did make a point of getting me to demonstrate some of the key skills involved in the work of a detective – but often Richard appeared to treat us as equals and to value Jonah's opinions as highly as mine. The experience stood me in good stead when I became a DI myself and had my own team to train up, but I couldn't help feeling that, as soon as I'd shown Jonah how to do something, he was given the same opportunities to exercise that skill as I was. I don't want to make a big thing of this, because in reality we all got on very well together, but it did sometimes seem that Jonah was being allowed to take on responsibilities that I wouldn't have been permitted to have so early on in my career.

I remember one case in particular. It was not long after

Jonah was transferred to CID. Up until then, I'd still been going out with Richard to view every crime scene and interview every witness, with Jonah coming along for the ride, to observe our technique and take notes. This time Richard had evidently decided that Jonah was ready to act as his assistant without me present as well – or maybe he just didn't have the manpower to spare. Whatever the reason, I remember being left in the office checking through files while Jonah went off with Richard to interview the mother of a girl who had gone missing. And I remember it crossing my mind that perhaps this was the beginning of the end for my partnership with Richard.

Looking back, I realise now that Richard was just helping us each to play to our strengths. Jonah was never going to have the patience to stick with going through mountains of paper to extract a small piece of information – or at least, not reliably. His attention would start to wander and he'd miss things. But he did have a real gift for leaps of the imagination that sometimes really pushed a case along when we were struggling to make sense of the evidence we had before us. Anyway, we rubbed along pretty well for quite some time and, though I say it myself, we notched up a good number of successes during that period. Probably our friendly competition for Richard's esteem and attention made both Jonah and me more effective – it kept us on our mettle and always striving to improve.

It didn't seem long before Jonah was promoted. When I check the dates, I can see that, in fact, it only took him just one year less to make the transition from constable to sergeant than it took me, but somehow it felt as if he had been with us for hardly any time before he had become my equal in rank. I began to wonder if I ought to start looking to move on, in order to make room for Jonah to supplant me as Richard's bag-carrier. However, no sideways moves presented themselves and Richard appeared content to continue with the two of us playing more or less equal, but different, roles in his team. And before long, it became obvious that Richard had plans for Jonah to move on up the greasy pole. Now that Richard was a Chief Inspector, he had set his sights on his most recent protégé reaching the rank of inspector.

To be fair to Richard, he also tried to persuade me to take the inspector's exams, but I've never been a great one for book learning, and sitting in an examination room terrifies me far more than tackling an armed criminal. So I kept putting it off, while Jonah – who is extremely bright and ought really to have gone to university – flew through the exams with top marks. And with DCI Richard Paige backing him, it was never going to be long before he got his promotion.

4. SEPARATE WAYS

A mere four years after reaching the rank of sergeant, Jonah successfully applied for an inspector's post in South Oxfordshire. It was more convenient geographically for him, now that Margaret had a consultant post in Reading, as well as being a step up. From my point of view, it meant that we no longer worked together on a daily basis. Occasionally our paths would cross – criminals have no respect for police service divisional boundaries! – but it was rare and more likely to involve telephone conversations than meeting face to face.

Things settled down into a comfortable routine. Richard continued to be a very hands-on detective and I continued to learn a lot from him. Jonah continued to cover himself in glory in his new role. We would sometimes hear about his exploits, and Richard would smile with quiet satisfaction at the thought that he had been responsible for spotting him and bringing him on. I fully expected him to be made a DCI any moment and had visions of eventually having him as my Chief Constable!

I just about managed to scrape through the inspector's exams before Jonah got his DCI post. Richard said that he was delighted at my promotion, but I couldn't help feeling that his congratulations were a bit muted compared with when Jonah moved up from sergeant. I rather fancy he may have thought that I wasn't really inspector material and would do better continuing in a more junior role. I have to say I wasn't sure myself if I was up to being in charge of an investigation. Angie told me that it was just that Richard would have liked to keep me as his assistant and was worrying about where he was going to find another decent detective sergeant. Of course, she was just trying to boost my confidence.

Jonah sent a very nice card congratulating me on my promotion – at least I think that's what it said! His handwriting was always impossible to decipher. We used to joke that he must have caught the knack for illegible handwriting from his wife, doctors being notorious for their untidy scrawls. It was good of him to take an interest – even if it did also serve to remind me that it had taken me twenty years to achieve what he had managed in eight. Of course, it was my own fault for being so diffident about putting myself forward, so I can't complain. If Richard hadn't pushed me, I'd probably have still been a sergeant when I retired.

I have to admit that I enjoyed the additional independence that being an inspector brought me – but I was glad that Richard was still there in the background to give me advice. He was still moving on an upward trajectory himself. When he became superintendent, it crossed my mind that maybe he'd got wind of his likely promotion and pressed me to take the inspector's exams to make sure I had somewhere to go when he moved on.

When one of Bernie's students looked to have hanged himself from the staircase of his college room, I happened to be the officer called to the scene. I rang Richard and told him about it before setting off and, to my surprise, he decided to come along too. I wonder if something in my tone of voice made him realise that there was something special about this call. I was very nervous of being the one in charge of the case because I knew that Bernie had experience of suicide before and I was afraid this might be difficult for her. I didn't tell Richard anything about that when I rang him – but he managed to get it out of me later. He was amazing at persuading people to tell him things without seeming to probe. Anyway, whatever the reason, he came along and took charge of what turned out to be a murder, rather than a suicide.

And, as I've described elsewhere, that was the start of the very strange relationship between Richard and Bernie that led to them getting married a couple of years later. Jonah wasn't at the wedding. Looking back, that's quite surprising really, because I know Richard was still keeping in touch with him and monitoring his progress. I don't know whether he invited Jonah and he couldn't come, or if he deliberately avoided inviting lots of old colleagues. There wasn't much police representation, now I come to think about it, so probably Jonah wasn't invited. I was Best Man – returning the favour from when Richard was my Best Man nearly twenty years earlier – and Angie and Hannah took the role of supporters of the bride. I won't say bridesmaids because, at Bernie's insistence, there was none of the usual dressing up in pretty frocks and carrying posies. I had charge of the ring; Hannah read a lesson; and Angie and I both signed the register.

Looking back now, I wonder whether one reason for Richard not inviting all his police colleagues to the ceremony was that he was afraid that Bernie's unconventionality would provoke a lot of comment among them. I can just imagine the sorts of things some of them might say about the idea of a bride dressed in trousers and no flowers at all. Jonah, I think, would probably have relished it – Margaret certainly would have done. After all, they went off on their honeymoon with Jonah riding pillion behind his new wife on her motorbike! Come to think of it, Bernie and Margaret were alike in many ways. Not in appearance at all, but in outlook. Neither of them had any regard at all for convention – or perhaps they took cognisance of it and then, if they didn't see any value in it, deliberately went out of their way to flout it.

After that, the next time I remember meeting Jonah was at Richard's funeral – but that had better wait for another chapter.

5. FRIENDS REUNITED?

I can remember the scene at Richard's funeral as if it were yesterday. Jonah accosted me at the reception in the church hall after the service and asked me to introduce him to the widow. I tried to make conversation, which wasn't that hard because it turned out he knew nothing at all about Bernie. I explained to him that she hadn't taken Richard's name when she married, so she was still Dr Bernadette Fazakerley. I think I was rather pleased to be able to say *Dr* Fazakerley because it showed Jonah that Richard's wife wasn't just anyone, by which I suppose I mean that she was a good as Jonah's wife, Margaret!

I can remember the exchange that Bernie had with Jonah word-for-word. I introduced him very formally – trying to distance myself from him and not give any indication that he had enjoyed any sort of special relationship with Richard. At first, Bernie replied equally formally.

'Pleased to meet you.' She said politely. 'It's amazing how many of Richard's colleagues have come to see him off. I had no idea he was so popular.'

'I owe him a lot. He took me on when I first joined the CID. He taught me all I know.'

That's probably the point at which Bernie recognised the name – Jonah isn't one that you come across every day – and started to remember Richard talking about him. I suppose he must have told her that one of his protégés had pulled off a coup recently and she saw it as an opportunity to move the conversation on from eulogising Richard and condoling his widow.

'I doubt that,' she said to him. 'Aren't you the officer who was responsible for clearing up that big fraud case? Richard would never have been any good with something like that – his command of even simple arithmetic was absolutely dire. A bent banker would easily have been able to run rings around him. What was the banker's name? It was something odd, I know – something weird and Welsh.'

'Merlin Price-Davies,' Jonah stammered out at last, after gathering his thoughts. That may well have been the first time I've seen him taken aback in a conversation. Trust Bernie to be capable of wrong-footing even the most self-possessed.

'That's the one,' she said, smiling. 'It makes you expect someone in a druid costume with long hair and a beard, but he turned out to be just some banker in a pinstriped suit who's probably never been out of the Home Counties. I gather it was quite a coup to get a conviction. You will obviously go far.'

'Oh, I don't know about that,' Jonah gave that annoying self-deprecating laugh that I always hated so much when we worked together. 'It wasn't all down to me. Anyway, I didn't come here to talk about my achievements. I wanted to tell you how sorry I was to hear about Richard's death and to say how much I owe to him.'

'And to see what sort of woman would marry him after all these years?' Bernie suggested – and I think I caught a wicked gleam in her eye as she said it.

'Since you mention it – I confess I was curious to meet you. Richard had been such a very confirmed bachelor – very much married to the job – and we were all rather taken aback to hear that he'd taken the plunge into matrimony at what you have to admit was a fairly advanced age. I mean – it would have to be someone rather special.'

Bernie never did take kindly to flattery, so she wasn't going to let him get away with that.

'Or maybe he was just desperate to ensure that he would be cared for in his declining years,' she suggested, deadpan.

'I'm quite sure that was not even a part of his considerations.' She had Jonah on the run now alright.

'You're probably right. He was generally quite astute,

and if that had been his aim, I'm sure that he could have found someone more suited to the role. I make no pretence of having a caring or sympathetic nature. So, if you are wondering why he married me, join the club – I certainly wouldn't have been foolish enough to sign up to living with me on a permanent basis!'

I couldn't help being amused at Jonah's discomfiture. He clearly didn't know how to follow this. 'Someone told me you were a don,' he said in the end, desperately trying to keep the conversation going.

'That's right,' Bernie nodded, magnanimously giving him a breather in the conversational sparring match. 'I'm Applied Mathematics Fellow at St Luke's College.'

'It must be the busiest time of the year for you, with all the new students starting. I hope you're allowed some time off, under the circumstances.'

'Well done! You didn't say it. I'm impressed.'

'Say what?'

'Usually at this point in the conversation, people give a little laugh and say, "I was never any good at Maths at school." And then they start looking for an opportunity to get away and talk to someone more interesting.'

'Ah! But I was always very good at Maths at school.'

I could see that they were hitting it off. Jonah and Bernie shared a lot of the same sense of humour and that must have started to come across even during this short acquaintance. I suppose I rather resented the way Jonah seemed to be making friends so easily with Bernie, when it had taken Angie and me so many years to break down the carapace that she'd erected in the immediate aftermath of Stephen's death. I couldn't help trying to take him down a peg.

'And at everything else, I'm sure,' I said, 'and doesn't he know it!'

'I must say,' Jonah went on, ignoring me, 'you aren't my idea of a typical Oxford don.'

'You mean,' grinned Bernie, 'I don't sound as if I went

to Roedean or Cheltenham Ladies College, and you're wondering how I ever came to be allowed into the Oxbridge establishment. Richard always used to say–'

Then she stopped short and we realised that she was staring at something on the other side of the hall, near the door.

'Look, I'm sorry,' she apologised hastily, 'Richard's mother is just leaving. I must see her off. Thank you for coming. Maybe we can speak again later.'

I saw Jonah watching her as she hurried off cross the room, weaving between the guests with mutters of apology. I decided to finish off the well-worn story that Bernie had been about to tell.

'Richard always used to say that when she was interviewed for her fellowship the panel asked at the end, "and now do you have any questions for us?" and she said, "Are youse giving me this job or what?" and none of them had the courage to say "no"!'

I don't suppose my attempt at a Liverpool accent was as amusing as it was intended to be. In any case, I'm not sure that Jonah was listening to me. He was more concerned with watching Bernie. Eventually he realised that I'd been speaking to him and he turned back to face me.

'How is she, d'you think?' he asked 'No tears. Putting a brave face on it d'you reckon?'

I was stung by the implication that perhaps Bernie wasn't all that sorry about Richard's death after all.

'Our Bernie doesn't show her emotions,' I told him sharply, 'but don't think for a moment she doesn't feel Richard's death very much.' I saw Jonah's surprised look and tried to think of something to tone down what I'd said and explain the situation more. 'She and Angela are very close – I think that's what's keeping her going at the moment, and of course she's been keeping busy with the funeral and everything.'

'Angela?' Jonah didn't seem to recognise the name.

'My wife.'

'Of course! I remember now.' Jonah seemed to be glad to be on safe ground again. 'And what about the children – you had two, didn't you – a boy and a girl?'

'Hannah's at university studying to be a nurse and Edward's in lower sixth.' I think we were probably both relieved to be able to fall back on the routine of catching up on one another's family news. I gabbled on, without thinking, just pleased to have something to say. 'We were afraid that he was going off the rails, but Bernie took an interest in him and persuaded him that he could indulge in his obsession with computers by doing a computer science degree. He finally knuckled down and actually did quite well in his GCSEs after all, which is a great relief to us all. I must say I don't envy Bernie having it all still to come – and on her own too.'

'What do you mean?' Jonah jumped on my throw-away remark. 'She and Richard didn't have any kids, did they?'

Too late, I realised that I had probably said more than I ought to have done – certainly a lot more than I intended to say. Jonah seems to have inherited Richard's knack of getting people to talk without the need for actually questioning them.

'Not yet,' I agreed. Then I lowered my voice so as not to broadcast what I was regretting having inadvertently revealed. 'I don't think I ought to be telling you this, but having said so much I'd better. Bernie's expecting.'

Jonah said nothing. He just looked at me as if he knew that there was more to come. I managed to keep silent for maybe half a minute and then I gave in.

'The thing is,' I went on, 'she didn't tell Richard before he died, and now she's racked with guilt. She didn't know how he would take it, you see. I don't think either of them had thought about the possibility, what with her just turned forty and him, well...'

'Getting on for sixty, I suppose.' Jonah looked thoughtful. Then he took my arm and moved closer, so that he could speak in my ear. 'Let me know when the baby's born – I'd like to ... send a card or something.'

Well, I could hardly say no, could I? And, having agreed, I felt honour bound to go through with it. So, about six months later, I dropped Jonah a line in an email to let him know about Lucy's arrival.

6. FRIEND OF THE FAMILY

He didn't just send a card. Bernie didn't say anything about it at the time, but we found out later that he came round one day to see the baby and bring a present. And that wasn't all. He also wrote a chapter for the book that Bernie was compiling of stories and pictures about Richard. Her idea was to have something to show to Lucy so that she would know something of what her father had been like.

We – Angie and I – didn't find out any of this until Lucy's first birthday came around. We went round for tea that day and found the whole of the living room floor taken up with a massive plastic toy railway. When we asked where it had come from, Bernie told us that Jonah had brought it. It had belonged to his two boys and he'd handed it on to Lucy. It was generous of him to think of Lucy instead of saving it for his own grandchildren. It was even more generous of him to have gone to so much trouble over the chapter he wrote for the book.

Bernie must have had the book out to show Jonah shortly before we arrived and it was still lying there when we entered the living room. Angie had a look inside to see if there were any new entries and you should have seen the pages that Jonah had written! I think I mentioned before that his handwriting was usually all over the place. I suppose, being left-handed made it difficult for him – that and always being in too much of a hurry to bother about little things like legibility. At first, I couldn't believe Bernie when she told me that he'd written the story himself. It was the most faultless calligraphy you've ever seen. I would never have thought him capable of such a work of art – except that, being Jonah Porter, he could do anything he set his mind to.

It must have taken him hours to complete. I wondered why he had bothered. It wasn't as if Lucy was likely to appreciate the difference compared with a word-processed document. I have to admit that I suspected at the time that it was largely showing off. He must have known that some of his old colleagues – me in particular – would see the book, and he wanted his contribution to be demonstrably the best. Now, I think I was probably wrong. I think he was genuinely trying to do something to show his appreciation of everything he owed to Richard.

I don't know why, but I have to admit to being rather resentful of Jonah showing an interest in Bernie and Lucy. After all, she'd chosen Angie and me for Lucy's godparents, not him. I was glad that he hadn't spent any money on Lucy's present. Maybe Bernie was right when she said that he was really just de-cluttering his loft. Looking back, I wonder if Bernie detected my antipathy towards Jonah. She certainly never went out of her way to tell us about his visits.

For the next eight years, Jonah would turn up, unannounced, every year on Lucy's birthday. Bernie tells me that she several times invited him to visit in between birthdays but he always declined. I suppose he was trying to maintain his mystique, by only appearing once a year and never making arrangements in advance. Typical Jonah! He was very good at ensuring that he was always the centre of attention.

Something else that I didn't find out about until after the event was that he was secretly helping Bernie in her quest to find out more about Richard's mother. I don't know if I told you that she mysteriously vanished when he was eight years old and then, just as mysteriously reappeared when he was in his forties. After she died (which was when Lucy was only a few months old), Bernie decided to try to find out why she had deserted her little boy all those years ago. Talk about a cold case! If she'd asked me about it, I'd have told her she was wasting her time trying to get to the bottom of things that happened half a century before.

I'll skim over the next five years, including Angie's death and my subsequent marriage to Bernie. I've talked about them elsewhere. Since this is about Jonah's relationship with my new family, I will just mention that Bernie invited him to our wedding and he sent his apologies. I can't remember now what it was that prevented him coming, but I do remember a feeling of relief that he wouldn't be there to upstage me in my moment of glory. I've often wondered what he thought of us getting hitched. I daresay he considered I wasn't good enough for her. Maybe that's why he didn't come to the wedding – or maybe he just wanted to maintain his mysterious once-a-year routine – or maybe he realised that his presence might somehow queer my pitch. It's no good asking him because he'd only insist that he had a prior engagement. He can be very stubborn about letting you know his true feelings sometimes.

Of course, now that I was Lucy's stepfather, as well as her godfather, I was usually around when Jonah made his annual birthday visits. To be fair to him, he was always very careful not to usurp my position.

I remember particularly Lucy's eighth birthday. We'd given her a new bicycle, of which she was very proud. Everyone cycles in Oxford and we'd been going on family rides together since she was small. However, I was still not happy with the idea of her going out on the road without Bernie or me accompanying her. Bernie disagreed, but she backed me up in front of Lucy. That, by the way, goes to show how much Bernie had changed compared with the way she behaved towards Richard when he wanted to protect her from potential dangers. She's mellowed a lot over the years and manages to accept – not always with good grace, but at least with good manners – that other people have a right to be genuinely concerned about her wellbeing.

However, to get back to Jonah: Lucy appealed to him over the business of the unfairness of parents and their insistence that she was too young to be allowed out on her own on a bicycle. He listened to her arguments very seriously – he always spoke to Lucy as if he were a Regency gentleman addressing a lady – and then told her equally seriously that she ought to be glad that she had people who were so concerned about keeping her safe, and that he wished his wife would listen to him when he asked her to be more careful riding her motorbike. That immediately deflected Lucy away from her grievance because she'd never come across the idea of a woman riding a motorbike and she immediately demanded proof that Jonah wasn't making it all up.

Lucy's ninth birthday was the last one to follow the established pattern. I have a home video of the day. I'd built her a tree house in the big oak tree in the back garden. Well, to be accurate, one of Bernie's university colleagues, Dr Martin Riess, had suggested that it was a perfect tree for a house and the two of us had made it together. Lucy was very excited about it and insisted on taking Jonah up into the tree to see it in all its glory. Then after that, he climbed down and she jumped down after him and allowed him to catch her in his arms. She did that a few times, laughing more and more on each repetition of the game. I felt a pang of jealousy that my stepdaughter was favouring a comparative stranger with so much attention – and so much trust. I think Bernie realised that and that's why she told Lucy that she ought to show more respect to our guest and give him a rest.

Then, a few weeks later everything changed for Jonah – and, as it turned out, for us too.

7. A SHOT IN THE DARK

Well, it wasn't really a shot in the dark – it was in broad daylight, as the saying goes. I've never quite worked out why daylight is described as *broad* but never mind. As you can hardly fail to be aware, one fateful day in the summer of 2009, DCI Jonah Porter was engaged in a spot of innocent gardening when an unknown gunman shot him in the back of the neck from behind the back fence of his South Oxfordshire home. The result was a lengthy stay in hospital, an even longer period of rehabilitation, and permanent disability.

Everyone who knew Jonah was totally shocked by the incident and its outcome. What made things worse was the contrast between Jonah before and after his injury. Several of his colleagues and ex-colleagues commented to me on the energy with which he used to attack each case, and how difficult it was going to be for him to adjust to life in a wheelchair. I think Paul Godwin summed it up very well a few years later when he described Jonah as having been *almost indecently energetic*[1]. I certainly remember him striding around a crime scene, poking his nose into everything and expecting everyone to jump to and get things done by yesterday!

The other thing that was very worrying for me and my police colleagues was the idea that there was a maniac out there gunning for police officers. As the days, weeks, and months stretched on, and we were no further forward in discovering the perpetrator, it seemed as if we might never know why Jonah had been targeted in this way. At first, it made us all very jumpy, but then, as always happens in this sort of situation, we settled down to the new reality and stopped watching anxiously for signs that there might be a gunman lurking in the bushes out to get us.

---

[1] You can read about Paul and the occasion when he said this in CHANGING SCENES OF LIFE.

Bernie and Lucy heard about it on the radio before I got home with the news, which had spread through the police force like wild fire. Lucy wanted to go and see him right away, but we persuaded her that she would have to wait until Jonah and his family were ready for visitors. Bernie rang Margaret, who must have been astonished to get a call from someone whom she could only have heard of at all as a very remote acquaintance. At least, that's how Bernie described it to me at the time; I wonder now exactly what Jonah had told Margaret about his birthday visits to Lucy. He must have had some sort of explanation as to why that day was sacrosanct.

I thought that we ought to keep out of it and let Jonah and his family come to terms with things in private. Bernie agreed, up to a point, but she also had Lucy's repeated questions to contend with. In the end, she went over on her own to see Jonah in hospital. She wanted to see how the land lay and whether it was feasible for Lucy to visit. Jonah was delighted to see her – I suppose any new visitor must have been welcome – and insisted that she bring Lucy as soon as she could. I wasn't sure that it was a good idea, but you can't say *no* to someone whose just been told he's likely to remain paralysed from the neck down for the rest of his life, can you?

When Lucy came back from her first visit, I thought at first that I'd been right. She was very subdued and Bernie found her crying in bed that night over the thought that Jonah was never going to get better again. I didn't want her to go again, but she'd come to an arrangement with one of the nurses on the ward that she was going to help by feeding Jonah and helping him to put back some of the weight he'd lost during the first weeks following his injury. So I was overruled on the grounds that she could not possibly go back on a promise.

Of course, it turned out that I was completely wrong. Lucy thrived in her new role as part of Jonah's nursing team, and she became much more cheerful now that she felt that she was doing something to help him. Getting him to eat his meals was only part of it. Before long, she was accompanying him on walks around the hospital grounds, as he got used to controlling an electric wheelchair. Bernie and Margaret were also getting on like a house on fire and even I started to look forward to visiting the hospital. In my case, it wasn't so much to see Jonah as to have the chance of talking to one of his nurses who was a Jamaican and loved chatting about her memories of the Caribbean and comparing them with my news of what Eddie was doing over there.

8. STUBBORN AS A MULE

It isn't in Jonah's nature to allow a little thing like being paralysed from the neck down to get in the way of him doing what he wants! As Lucy's tenth birthday approached, he made it clear that he was determined that he was going to turn up at our house with a present for her, exactly as he had done every year since she was born. I think that he would have liked to have organised it without reference to us, so as to appear out of the blue the way he always used to, but Margaret insisted that Bernie had to be involved, seeing as it might require her house to have alterations done, to enable his wheelchair to get inside. Besides, it was one thing for Jonah to arrive unannounced, it was quite another to have him rolling up accompanied by Margaret and some of the nursing staff from the ward to take care of him.

I'll never forget Lucy's face when she came in from school and saw him there in our living room. And even I felt a lump come into my throat when she opened up the birthday card that he'd bought her and saw that he'd managed to scrawl a message to her himself. Actually, the writing wasn't that much worse than it always used to be before his injury, but now it was a much bigger achievement because he had managed it with only his first two fingers and thumb. Lucy still has that card tucked away in the drawer next to her bed. It's a symbol that Jonah wasn't going to take things lying down and was still a force to be reckoned with.

It's also a symbol of how much Lucy means to him and I'm surprised really that, for the first time, I didn't feel at all resentful of him taking such an interest in her – and the way she made it clear that she looked forward to seeing him. At one level, you're probably saying to yourself that it isn't that odd because how could I be jealous of a man who's almost completely paralysed and dependent on other people? But that's not the point. I've come to realise that Jonah never was any threat to my relationship with Lucy – or Bernie, come to that. I suppose it all started out with him wanting to do something to show his appreciation for what Richard did for him – no, it wasn't as calculated as that; it was more about wanting to demonstrate his esteem for Richard. And then, like practically every adult who ever met Lucy, he fell in love with the little girl. I hope it's nothing to do with her blue eyes and golden curls – Bernie would go ballistic if she thought that was what attracted everyone to her daughter! – but I have a suspicion that those things do help. It's a wonder she didn't become a spoilt brat, with everyone fawning over her the way we do, but then, it's probably the fact that she never appears aware of how much everyone admires her that keeps us all in her thrall.

Getting back to Jonah, the birthday outing was just a preliminary to his return home from the hospital, which happened gradually over a period of a couple of months. As soon as he was home, in the care of Margaret and their younger son, Nathan, with help from some professional agency staff, he started talking about getting back to work. Reactions to his stated intention of returning to his DCI job ranged from incredulity through laughter to anxiety that he was in denial and would suffer when he realised that his hopes could never be fulfilled. Within the police service, there was initially an assumption that he would take early retirement, and senior officers were completely wrong-footed when he insisted that he wanted to come back to his old job. However, he was persistent and they had to listen and to start thinking of reasons for refusing his request – which wasn't that hard really.

I could see both points of view. I understood Jonah's determination not to allow himself to be thrown on the scrapheap, and I shared his love of the job itself; but I could also see why people found it hard to see how he was going to manage it in his current state – or why he would want to try. It came as no surprise to me that senior officers struggled to see how a man with Jonah's disabilities could possibly succeed in a profession that traditionally required a minimum level of physical fitness. Moreover, he was fifty-two, and many police officers retire at fifty-five as a matter of course, so it was only natural to imagine that he would take the offer of an enhanced pension and go quietly. Some of his colleagues actually said to his face that they envied him being able to retire early and they wished they could afford to do so – which just shows how lacking in imagination they were.

What they failed to appreciate was how different it is to choose to retire from being told that you have to go. Effectively, what they were saying to Jonah was that he was now useless and that he ought to hide himself away in a nice comfortable care home somewhere out of sight and let other people look after him. Most people, when they retire, take up new hobbies or voluntary work and do all the things they never had time for when they were working. Jonah wasn't in a position to take up new activities. His main hobby had been gardening, which was quite impossible in his condition – apart from in an advisory capacity, which he does very well now, but that's another story! So I could completely understand why he needed to prove that he could still contribute to society and that he would want it to be by returning to being a full-time detective.

Jonah's son, Nathan, was positioned right at the extreme of the anxious end of the spectrum. His father's injury hit him very badly and he became very protective of him. He got quite angry with Margaret and Bernie when they wouldn't back him in trying to persuade Jonah to give up his campaign to be reinstated. He thought that it was unkind to allow Jonah to continue deluding himself that he could get back to normal life and to his old job. Looking back, I think we could probably have been more understanding towards the boy, but we were all more concerned with helping Jonah come to terms with his disability. I'm afraid that Nathan's attitude drove a wedge between him and Jonah, which they've found difficult to shift.

With Bernie on Jonah's side, the police authorities had no chance of winning the argument. When she sets her mind to getting something, it's pointless trying to oppose her for long – not that Jonah isn't a formidable force to be reckoned with in his own right! It took a good few months, but eventually the powers that be succumbed to the inevitable and granted Jonah a trial period of three months to prove that he could still do the job. Five years on, he's still there and still irrepressibly enthusiastic about tackling each new case.

9. CHANGE OF CIRCUMSTANCES

2013 was a very significant year for all of us. It marked a turning point in the relationship between Jonah's family and ours. It started off with a call from Jonah, asking if one of us could go with him on a trip up to Shropshire. He'd had a call from West Mercia police suggesting that a body that had been found in the woods up there might be connected with a series of murders that he was investigating in Oxfordshire. He had agreed to go up there over the weekend, forgetting that his professional carer wasn't booked to work beyond Friday afternoon. Margaret was on call that weekend, so he turned to us. I'd retired by then and I think he thought it would do me good to get involved in a bit of police work to stop my mind going to mush! However, I had my hands full that weekend with my Granddaughter, Emily. I'd offered to have her to stay for a few days to give Hannah a break. She was heavily pregnant with Amber at the time and getting very tired and run down.

I can't remember who suggested it first, but the upshot of that telephone call was that Bernie went off to Shropshire with Jonah and a whole new phase of our life began.

The officer in charge of the Shropshire case was Paul Godwin, who, by coincidence, had worked previously both with Jonah and, more recently, with me, before being transferred to West Mercia. Jonah hadn't mentioned his name on the phone, so it was a complete surprise to Bernie when she recognised him sitting in the hotel in Oswestry waiting for them. There's no reason why Jonah should have known that Paul worked with me after he left Jonah's team – and still less reason why he should have known that he had become rather a favourite with Bernie. Still, it was a bit of a shock for her to see him sitting there. And, as it turned out, it was even more of a shock for poor Paul to see Jonah arriving in a wheelchair. He'd somehow

managed not to hear about Jonah having been shot –
although it had been on the national, as well as the local,
news and had spread through the police grapevine like
nobody's business.

The other thing that Paul found shocking was the idea
that Bernie was not only sharing a room with Jonah but
seeing to all his most intimate needs. Like many people, he
expected me to be upset at the thought of my wife
dressing and undressing another man, not to mention
washing him and toileting him. It's funny when you think
that nobody ever questioned it being OK for Angie to be
working on a male ward with any number of patients,
some of whom were a great deal younger and more good-
looking than Jonah!

This story isn't about Paul or I might tell you about the
way his sergeant – a bright girl by the name of Karen
Evans – got hold of the wrong end of the stick and
thought that there was something going on between
Bernie and Paul. Or I might go on to tell you about how,
after a while, Paul and Karen teamed up domestically as
well as in the workplace and have recently announced their
intention of getting married.

The important thing from the point of view of Jonah's
relationship with us is that it opened Bernie's eyes to the
idea of a complete change to her career. This was the first
time she'd had hands on experience of a live police
investigation and she caught the bug and wanted more
after it was over. I think that her job at the university had
been starting to pall for some time and she'd been toying
with the idea of early retirement – originally with a view to
spending more time with Lucy, but now with something
else in mind altogether. By the time they'd got back from
Shropshire, she'd proposed to Jonah that she should
become his Personal Assistant, in place of the agency staff
that he'd been using up until then.

Jonah jumped at the idea – as well he might. I won't
say anything against the professional carers, because they

were very good in many ways and did a splendid job at looking after Jonah physically. However, I could see the change in him after Bernie took over. It made all the difference to Jonah having someone looking after him who was his own intellectual equal. It also made things easier that he knew that Bernie was as committed as he was to getting the job done. Above all, it made a difference knowing that her interest in him was more than simply as a professional carer.

10. OUTRAGEOUS FORTUNE

It's strange the way when things start going wrong for someone they often go from bad to worse. Up until 2009, I would have said that Jonah had led something of a charmed life, with everything going right for him and his family. An amazing stroke of luck had brought him to the attention of DCI Richard Paige, starting him on a career in the CID that looked to be moving him ever onwards and upwards towards Chief Constable or whatever goal he may have set himself. He was married to a highly intelligent – if a little eccentric – woman, who was also a skilled surgeon and bringing in a consultant surgeon's salary. They had a house in South Oxfordshire with extensive grounds in which he could indulge his passion for gardening. Their two sons both went off to good universities and seemed set to make successful professional careers for themselves. If anybody ever had it all, it was Jonah Porter.

The bullet in his neck changed everything. I still find it hard to fathom how he managed to come through that without sinking into despondency and despair – not least, because it was so much against his nature to be inactive or reliant on other people. I'm sure that his wife, Margaret, must have played a big part in keeping him sane, particularly in the early days. And, of course, it was she upon whom he depended totally when they were at home together. So it must have come as an almost unbearable second blow when she was diagnosed with terminal cancer.

There have been massive advances in cancer treatment in recent years, but ovarian cancer is still very often a killer. The symptoms aren't that easy to spot in its early stages – and I don't imagine that Margaret was focussing on her own health under the circumstances of having Jonah's wellbeing to think about all the time. So, by the time she found out, there was nothing much that could be done. Surgery and chemotherapy put off the inevitable for a few months, but we all knew that there would be no cure.

If I believed in God, I would be very angry with him for allowing it to happen. It seemed such a waste for Margaret to die when there was so much for her still to do. Quite apart from looking after Jonah, she was saving lives on a daily basis in her work in the emergency department at the hospital. I remember calling in at her office once and seeing the array of cards on the shelves – from grateful patients thanking her for patching them up after they'd damaged themselves in accidents of all kinds.

I think it was particularly hard for their two boys. Reuben, who had just qualified as a consultant and was settled with his wife and three kids in County Durham, was spared the agony of watching his mother's daily slow decline, but – which was quite possibly worse – he had to endure the impotence of following the progress of the disease from a distance, unable to do anything to help. Nathan, their younger son, had already been through the trauma of watching Jonah's slow rehabilitation while he was still at university. Now he was working to qualify as a barrister in London, which meant that he was close enough to come home virtually every weekend. He was – and is – very willing, but Jonah was never completely at ease with him taking on Margaret's role as principal carer.

Seeing how difficult it was for the family coming to terms with Margaret's inexorable decline and inevitable death, I began to wonder if I had been lucky to lose Angie suddenly and unexpectedly the way I did.

Margaret was incredibly brave – or at least that's how it appeared to us as outsiders. Of course, only she knows what agonies she went through as the disease ran its devastating course. And only Jonah knows what they may have confided to one another in those dreadful months leading up to her death. I just remember her being very calm and matter-of-fact, as if dying were just one of those inconveniences that you had to work around in your plans – like road closures or the office computer being off for routine maintenance.

The one thing that really did worry Margaret was what was going to happen to Jonah after she was gone. She told Bernie how pleased she was about her plan to take early retirement in order to become his Personal Assistant during working hours. That at least made a statement about his determination to continue working, but it was more difficult to decide what to do about caring for him at home. Paying for live-in professional staff was clearly an option, but as soon as the family admitted that they were unable to cope, there would be subtle pressure for Jonah to give up the family home and move into a care home, where the costs would be lower and the care could be delivered more efficiently.

They very sensibly called a family conference – Reuben and his wife Anne, Nathan, Jonah's sister, Sarah, and the three of us: Bernie, Lucy and myself. Reuben and Sarah both thought that it was odd including us, but Jonah and Margaret insisted. Reuben's first suggestion was that Jonah should give up the job and go up to Durham to live with them. His argument was that, since they already had to organise childcare for three kids, it would be relatively simple to work their lives around caring for him as well. When Jonah insisted that he wanted to stay in Oxfordshire in order to keep on working, Reuben and Sarah both thought that a care home would be the best option. Nathan volunteered to live at home and commute into London for his work, so that he could care for Jonah, but Margaret was sceptical that he would be able to cope and worried that his career might suffer.

All the time that members of Jonah's family were talking, I could see that Lucy was wanting to jump in to protest at the way everyone appeared to be assuming that looking after Jonah was a problem – or at very least a regrettable necessity – that needed to be addressed. She has always been very definite that caring for Jonah is, as far as she's concerned, a privilege and not a chore. Perhaps it's because, being only nine when it happened, she had never before had the experience of being entrusted with the care of another human being. She is rightly very proud of what she does for Jonah. I suspect that Bernie's attitude may have something to do with it as well. She grew up with a disabled mother and sees caring as just part of normal family life.

Even before Lucy burst in and interrupted the discussion, I'd been trying to think of a way that we might be able to offer help without stepping on the toes of Jonah's 'real' family. I can't remember now whether I'd got things worked out in advance or if it just occurred to me at the time. What I do want to put on record is that it wasn't something that Bernie and I cooked up together – still less that she was pressurising me to do it. Really, I couldn't see that there was anything else I could have done. No, that's coming across all wrong. I don't mean that I felt under an obligation or anything like that. I suppose what I'm getting at is that I wanted to help and I knew that Bernie and Lucy did too, but I also knew that Bernie wouldn't volunteer us to do anything in case she forced me into something I wasn't comfortable with. So it was down to me to make the first move. I don't know whether any of that makes sense, but that's how it was.

My proposal was that Jonah would come to stay with us during the working week, which made a whole lot of sense considering that Bernie was already committed to caring for him during working hours. Each weekend, he'd go back to the family home and Nathan would come out from London to stay with him. That way Nathan wouldn't have to commute daily and would be available for the various evening events that seem to be an important part of the life of an aspiring barrister. We'd had Jonah to stay several times before – particularly since Margaret had been ill – and our house had been modified in a number of ways to suit his needs. It seemed to me to be a perfect solution.

Jonah and Margaret agreed. I could see how relieved

they both were that Jonah would not be left entirely in Nathan's hands. Poor Nathan! He tries so hard, but it's difficult for Jonah to accept the reversal of roles involved in allowing his own son to look after all his bodily needs. And Nathan doesn't seem to be able to get over his tendency to over-protectiveness. Maybe when he has children of his own, he'll start to understand the concept of benign neglect!

People sometimes seem to think that I was being very noble and self-sacrificing, but I really didn't do anything special. In some ways, having Jonah living with us during the week made our life easier than when Bernie was having to drive over to his house each day to pick him up and take him to work and then drop him off again each evening before returning home. Jonah managed to get a transfer from South Oxfordshire to Oxford City, which means that now their travel to work distance is negligible and Bernie's working day is considerably shorter. Weekends were better too, because Lucy got plenty of opportunity to talk to Jonah in the evenings and stopped demanding to go over to visit him at home.

Margaret died shortly before Easter, just over a year after she was diagnosed. I remember that we buried her on Maundy Thursday. Jonah was with her in the hospice during her last hours and Bernie was with them when she died. I know I shouldn't have done, but I remember when I heard about it thinking how lucky Jonah was to have had the chance to say goodbye – in contrast to my own experience when Angie was killed.

11. REGIME CHANGE

Sharing Jonah's care with Nathan worked out fine for a while, but it wasn't long before the cracks began to show. As Margaret had foreseen only too well, Jonah found being cared for by Nathan somewhat trying – which was sad, because they are both wonderful people and it ought to be possible for them to get along. In fact, it isn't a matter of not getting along; it's just that Nathan is a bit too conscientious and tries too hard. He also worries too much about what might happen to his dad if he were to be left with nobody keeping an eye on him. Jonah did his best not to complain; he knew that his son was only being over-protective because he cared about him. However, I'm sure he sometimes felt that Nathan was being rather patronising.

Nathan for his part did his best not to get angry with Jonah for taking unnecessary risks and refusing to accept his limitations. I really feel for the boy, because it must be hard in his situation to know what to say when his father insists on doing some of the really ridiculous things that Jonah does sometimes do. It's much easier for me, being seven years older than him and having been his senior officer, back in the day. I do sometimes have to pull Jonah up about not taking proper care of himself, which I think I have a perfect right to do because, if he makes himself ill, we'll all suffer.

Secondly, there was Nathan's romance with Georgia, which provided a distraction from caring for his dad and a reason for him wanting to spend more time in London and less in rural Oxfordshire. She's another young would-be barrister at his chambers. Her father is a solicitor with a practice in Hertfordshire.

Georgia was – and still is – very understanding about Nathan's role, and never tried to prevent him from going home at weekends, but you could see that he was thinking about her – and about getting back to her – all the time he was with Jonah. It's better now that they're engaged, so that Georgia feels that she's part of the family and can help, instead of just keeping out of the way and not complaining about Nathan's time being taken up with caring for his father. She's Jewish, which may explain why she's so understanding of the concept of duty towards one's family – or is that just me revealing my own prejudices and repeating an ethnic stereotype?

Nevertheless, his love life, coupled with the demands of his work, which sometimes required attendance at evening meetings or legal dinners and sometimes involved travelling to see clients in other parts of the country, meant that Nathan occasionally had to ask us to keep Jonah at our house over the weekend as well as during the week. We were happy to have him and he enjoyed being able to watch Lucy playing in her football team, which often had matches on a Saturday afternoon, and joining in with our 'Saturday night cabaret', where we get a few friends round and have a singsong. I don't like to boast about our family life, but I think it was all a bit of a contrast with Jonah and Nathan sitting at home trying to make conversation!

Then, there was the garden. I think I mentioned that Jonah had always been a keen gardener. Of course, he was no longer in a position to take care of the large garden at his family home and Nathan did not have either the skill or the time to do so. They paid someone to come in regularly to mow the lawns and cut the hedges, but nothing more than routine maintenance. We could see that Jonah was frustrated at seeing the garden that he had designed and developed over so many years going into a decline, but we didn't have the time to help either.

To cut a long story short, we all agreed that it would be better for Jonah to move in with us full-time and to sell the family home in South Oxfordshire. Nathan and Georgia still help out – when we want to go away for a few days, for example – but he doesn't need to feel obliged to keep every weekend free to look after his dad. The house sale has put money in the bank for the future – disabled living doesn't come cheap! – as well as enabling us to buy some equipment to improve Jonah's quality of life now. I also believe that it's better for Jonah not to be staying in the house where he'd been happy with Margaret and constantly being reminded of her. I remember how difficult it was for me after Angie died, always half-expecting her to come out of the kitchen or the bedroom and join me.

So, here we are, a family of four: Bernie, Lucy, Jonah and me!

12. Conclusion

Before I finish, I just want to make something clear. People often seem surprised that I don't resent having Jonah living with us. They seem to think that I should be jealous of another man taking up so much of my wife's (and stepdaughter's) time, and they particularly worry about the idea of Bernie dressing and undressing him and sometimes sleeping in his room to take care of him during the night. All of that is pure nonsense and fails to understand the situation.

I suppose, if I'm honest, part of the reason that I was happy to take Jonah into our home – and before that I was happy for Bernie to give up her job to become his daytime assistant – is that Bernie is not – and she knows that she is not – the love of my life. I daresay my reaction would have been quite different if Angie and I had still been married and she had suggested bringing one of her patients home to live with us. I love Bernie, but I don't feel the same exclusive passion for her that I did – and still do – for Angie.

The other reason is also the reason for my choice of title for this section of my reminiscences, and it goes right back to those early days working under DI Richard Paige. When Jonah came on the scene, for me it was like having to share a parent with a troublesome younger brother. When he moved down to South Oxfordshire, it was like the kids leaving home. And now we're like grown up brothers who don't any longer need to be constantly proving that we're better than one another – or not often, anyway!

WITNESS
EVIDENCE

(A cautionary tale for police officers and juries.)

1 INTRODUCTION

You would think that the easiest crimes to solve would be the ones where you have several eyewitnesses who saw what happened and are willing to tell the police about it. However, often they can be the trickiest of all, because people can be amazingly bad at seeing what's really going on and at remembering what they saw. Sometimes when you read different eye-witness accounts of an incident and compare them, you are tempted to believe that they must be talking about completely different events.

This is an example of the sort of thing I mean. It took place not long before I retired from the police. I didn't get called in to lead the investigation until after half a dozen or so witnesses had already come down to the station and given their statements. It had all seemed very straightforward initially – quite within the capability of an experienced detective sergeant such as Anna Davenport – until she started comparing the statements taken by different officers on the team. She soon realised that any half-decent defence lawyer would be able to tear the prosecution case apart if we were to go ahead with charging the man we currently had in custody, based solely on the eye-witness evidence.

On the face of it, we had a very straightforward mugging. A young woman is walking across the University Parks on a Saturday afternoon. A man – homeless and known to the police for having caused a nuisance by being drunk in public on more than one occasion – trips her up, pounces on her, steals her purse from her bag and runs off. Members of the public come to her aid. Two young men – members of a college rowing team – pursue her attacker and bring him down with a rugger tackle. The purse is found later, abandoned in amongst some bushes along the path that the man took when he ran away.

As you can imagine, we were all feeling quite pleased with ourselves at first. PC Gavin Hughes, not one of our more dynamic officers, made the arrest. This was an unusual occurrence for him and we were all pleased for him because there had been murmurings on high that he needed to up his game in that respect. For that matter, the whole division had been under pressure to improve our clear-up statistics and this was a very welcome addition to a not over-long list of solved crimes that quarter. However, it turned out to be a good thing we looked into things more carefully, as you'll see.

I've written down the statements as best I can remember them – but of course, I've changed the names of the witnesses, suspects and victim. Read them for yourself and see what you make of them.

2 Statement by Ms Joanne Rowland, student at Wolfson College, taken by DC Andrew Lepage

I was walking back to my room in college from visiting a friend at St Catherine's College. I went across the Parks, because that is the shortest way. I went along the path that goes straight across the parks from St Cross Road to the alleyway to Norham Gardens. I was about half way when something tripped me up and I fell to the ground. The next thing I knew someone was leaning over me and holding on to me. I could smell alcohol on his breath. I panicked and tried to push him away. I think I screamed out at him to get off me, but I may just have wanted to scream.

I did not notice the man, whom I have now been told is Michael Lambert, until after he tripped me, but afterwards I saw a bench next to the path, right by where I'd fallen. I think he must have been sitting on the bench and when I went past, he put his foot out and tripped me up. I had never seen him before, but one of the people who came to help me said that they had seen him sitting there before and that they always used a different path when they saw him there because they did not like the look of him.

Two young men ran over. They were in running kit. I found out afterwards that they were called Mark Sanders and Thomas Caldwell and they were running in the Parks as part of their training for the Oriel College rowing team. They must have seen that I was in trouble. When Michael Lambert saw them, he got up and ran off. I think he was kneeling down beside me before that. There were other people coming to help by then, so Sanders and Caldwell ran after him.

Someone helped me up, and someone else picked up my phone, which had got kicked under the bench. I sat down on the bench. I had a bag over my shoulder with my purse in it. Someone saw it was open and told me to check it. I looked inside and saw that my purse was gone. People started looking around under the seat and in among the bushes for the purse.

Someone must have phoned for the Police, because a police officer in uniform came up and asked what had happened. I started to tell him, but then Sanders and Caldwell came back holding Lambert between them. They told the police officer that they had caught him as he was running away. Someone said something about my purse and the police officer asked him if he had taken it. He seemed to know Lambert quite well and used his first name when he spoke to him. Lambert muttered something. Then the police officer said he needed to search him, but before he could do it, someone shouted from over near the bushes by where the path crosses the other path, the one that goes along the back of the houses in Norham Gardens. One of them ran over to us and said that they had found a purse in the bushes. They said they had not picked it up in case it had fingerprints on it.

Some more police officers came and one of them showed me the purse. It was mine. I cannot remember how much money was in it, but I think it was still all there.

3 STATEMENT BY MR MARK SANDERS, STUDENT AT ORIEL COLLEGE, TAKEN BY DC ANDREW LEPAGE

I was out running with my friend Thomas Caldwell. We had been running for, approximately twenty minutes when we saw a woman walking along the path ahead of us. She was walking quite slowly down the middle of the path, but meandering a bit from side to side. I remember wondering if we might find it difficult to get past her. Then, all of a sudden, she fell over. Then I noticed a man sitting on a bench by the side of the path. I found out afterwards – when he was arrested – that his name was Lambert. He sort of pitched forward on top of the woman. We ran faster to get to her to help. The man must have seen us coming because he got up and ran off. So we chased him and caught him and brought him back. We handed him over to the police, who arrested him.

We hung around for a while and then the police asked us to come down and make a statement about what we saw.

4 Statement by Mr Thomas Caldwell, student at Oriel College, taken by DC Monica Philipson

I was out running with my friend Mark Sanders. We like to run a figure of eight round the parks, which means that we go along the central path twice. We saw a man in dirty clothes sitting on the bench where the incident took place the first time we passed it. The second time round, we saw a woman in her twenties – we heard afterwards that she was a doctoral student from Wolfson called Joanne Rowland – walking along the path. We only saw her from behind. When she got to the bench, the man put out his foot and tripped her up and she fell over. Right away the man – Lambert – was on top of her and she was screaming for help. We ran as fast as we could to get to her. When he saw us coming, he got up and ran away, so we gave chase and brought him down, in amongst the line of trees at the back of Norham Gardens.

We held on to him between us and frogmarched him back to the bench. By the time we got there, the police had arrived. They arrested him and took him away to the police station.

There were lots of people standing around, wanting to see that Ms Rowland was all right. Someone shouted out that they had found a purse. We all stood around talking for a while. We were going to go back to our run, but one of the police officers asked us to go to the police station with them and make a statement, which is what we did.

5 STATEMENT BY MS KATHERINE OAKSHOTT, STUDENT AT OXFORD HIGH SCHOOL, TAKEN BY DC MONICA PHILIPSON (IN THE PRESENCE OF HER FATHER)

We (Aimee Whitley and I) had been shopping in town. We came back across the parks. We went along the path by the river and the pond and then turned left to go along to the Norham Gardens entrance. We heard some people shouting and looked over see what was happening. We saw a man on the ground attacking a girl in a blue dress. Some men were running towards him, shouting – two of them, I think, but there may have been more.

He got up off the ground and ran off and the other men ran after him. They ran across in front of us. The first man threw something into the bushes. Then the other men caught up with him and grabbed him and they all fell on the ground. Then the two other men pulled the first man up and dragged him back along the path to the bench. We hung around by the path, wondering what to do and if we ought to say anything about the thing the man threw in the bushes.

There was more shouting and more people came running over to where we were. Someone said that the man had stolen the girl's purse, so then we said about him throwing something in the bushes. Everyone started looking and Aimee found it. We knew we shouldn't touch it because of fingerprints, so I got out the plastic bag that the DVD I'd bought was in and put my hand inside like a glove and picked it up like that. I carried it back to where there was a crowd of people round the bench with the girl sitting on it.

There were some police officers in uniform standing there, so I gave it to one of them. They asked us some questions and then Aimee and I went home. Later on, my Dad brought me down to the police station to make this statement.

6 STATEMENT BY MS AIMEE WHITLEY, STUDENT AT OXFORD HIGH SCHOOL, TAKEN BY DS ANNA DAVENPORT (IN THE PRESENCE OF HER MOTHER)

We were coming back from town along the path by the river. We turned left by the pond. Just after that, I saw some men running and I heard shouting and I looked across the grass and saw a whole lot of people standing around a bench. Then three men ran across in front of us and I saw one of them throw something small into the bushes. We stopped and wondered what to do. The men were hidden in the trees. I could hear sounds come from there and then the men came back out. The two in running gear were holding the other one by his arms and pulling him along.

I heard a police siren and a police car drew up in Parks Road and two uniformed officers got out and came across to the group by the bench. I said to Katie that we ought to tell someone about the man throwing something in the bushes, so we started to go over there to talk to the police. But then some people came towards us shouting out something about a woman's purse being stolen; so we started hunting in the bushes for it. Katie found it and she picked it up very carefully with a plastic bag round her hand. We took it to the police and they put it in an evidence bag.

The policeman talked to us and took our names, but he said he couldn't interview us formally without our parents being there. So we went home then.

7 The case so far

There were about a dozen more statements, from other members of the public who came over to help at the time or who contacted the station afterwards when they heard about it on the local radio or read about it in the Oxford Times. They were all pretty consistent about what happened – too consistent in some cases. It was clear that some accounts had been influenced by witnesses talking amongst themselves during the confused period while everyone was milling around by the bench, waiting for the police and then, afterwards, waiting for the purse to be found. The statements from those who came forward after reading the news reports clearly owed much to what had been written in the report on the Oxford Times website.

People usually think that the reason the police don't like letting the public know details of a case before the perpetrator has been convicted is that we're afraid that it will give suspects information that will help them to tell convincing lies – or else that we're worried about copycat offending that will obscure the main investigation – or maybe time-wasters pretending to have witnessed something when they didn't. In fact, usually what is a lot more important is the effect that hearing about, or reading about, or discussing an incident has on the memories of perfectly honest witnesses who only want to help.

Take this case, for instance. If you had been one of the hundreds of people walking in the parks that afternoon and you had seen a kerfuffle going on across the grass from where you were, and seen a couple of beefy young men chasing a tramp, you might well have thought nothing much of it. But then, when you read a day or two later that at woman has been assaulted by a homeless man in the parks and that two have-a-go heroes gave chase and wrestled him to the ground, you start to think that must have been what you saw last Saturday afternoon. And then, when you read that the homeless man tripped the woman up and then stole her purse from her bag while she was lying helpless on the ground, you start picturing the incident in your mind. And before you know where you are, your actual memory of the event (which is really very sketchy indeed) has been overwritten in your head by your imagined picture prompted by reading the report. Then, if you're a good citizen – or if you rather fancy yourself giving evidence in court – you toddle off down to the local nick and ask to make a statement.

Of course, none of you would allow your imagination to run riot like that, but plenty of perfectly honest people do.

DS Davenport – Anna – was fairly certain that Michael Lambert had stolen the woman's purse and then thrown it away when he got scared that he was going to be caught, but she was not completely satisfied that the stories that she had on file told the whole truth. Moreover, even if they were accurate, she knew that a good defence team would find a forensic psychologist willing to give expert evidence that the witness statements were contaminated by what is called in the jargon *co-witnessing*. That means that witnesses may have been influenced by hearing what other witnesses said about the incident when they made their own statements. For example, the two schoolgirls, Aimee and Katie, admit to having talked together during the incident, and will almost certainly have discussed it further on their way home and probably at home as well. They also heard what other people were saying about what happened. This means that what they said is really a joint statement, so the fact that their two accounts are very similar doesn't make it more likely to be accurate than if we only had evidence from one of them.

There was quite sufficient evidence, however, to keep Lambert in for questioning. Anna decided to interview him, adopting a non-confrontational approach in the hope that, if he relaxed he might tell them more than if he was constantly on the defensive. She also had in mind the need to make sure that if he were to confess there would be no chance that he might retract it later and claim that he had been put under duress. She's a very good officer and manages to think beyond simply getting enough evidence to charge a suspect. It's all too easy to build a case that then falls apart when you get to court.

8 INTERVIEW WITH MR MICHAEL LAMBERT,

UNEMPLOYED

Present: Michael Lambert [ML], DS Anna Davenport [AD], DC Andrew Lepage [AL], Justin Osgood LLB [JO] (Duty Solicitor)

AD: For the tape: you are Mr Michael Lambert, currently living in the homeless hostel on Woodstock Road – is that correct?

ML: Yes.

AD: This afternoon you were involved in an incident in the University Parks. I want you to tell me, in your own words, what happened.

ML: I was just sitting there minding my own business when this bird comes along, teetering on her high heels and tapping away on her phone. She isn't looking where she's going. I'm not surprised when she falls over and the phone goes flying. She was lying there, right in front of me, so I gets down beside her to help up. That's all I was doing – trying to help. She starts screaming and hitting me and then some big beefy blokes start running up and shouting at me and I think it's time I was out of there. So I run off. I hadn't done nothing – I just wanted to get away before they beat me up.

AD: I see. You say the woman fell over right in front of you. Did you see what made her fall?

ML: Like I said, she wasn't looking where she was going.

AD: Do you mean that she tripped over something?

ML: Yeah … I suppose so.

AL: Your foot maybe?

ML: No! I never touched her. She just fell.

AD: OK. Never mind about that. You said you got down to help her. Did you say anything to her to let her know that was what you were doing?

ML: Can't remember. I think I said, 'want a hand?' or

something like that.

AD: She had a bag over her shoulder. Did you notice that?

ML: No. And I didn't take nothing out of it neither.

AD: If you were only trying to help, why did you run off when the two men came up?

ML: She was screaming and hitting me. I wanted to get away. No-one would of believed me. You don't either, do you?

AD: I'm trying to, Michael. But we can't help you if you don't answer our questions.

SILENCE

AD: Tell me what happened next, Michael.

ML: Like I said, I run off. And these blokes come after me and knocked me down and dragged me back to where the bird was sitting, with all these people standing round her yacking. And then Gav Hughes, he come up and arrested me. But I ain't done nothing.

AD: We have witnesses who saw you throw something away as you ran. What was it?

ML: It weren't nothing. I never threw nothing. They're lying.

AL: You're sure about that? You didn't have anything in your hand when you ran off – I don't know, a sandwich that you were eating, maybe?

ML: I told you – I didn't throw nothing in no bushes. I know that's where you found the bird's purse, but I never threw it there. I never took it.

AD: We didn't say you did, Michael. We're just trying to find out what happened. Now, please think again. What was it that you threw away as you ran?

PAUSE WHILE THE SUSPECT CONFERS WITH THE DUTY SOLICITOR

AD: Are you ready to tell us what it was that you threw into the bushes by the path?

ML: It wasn't the bird's purse – or anything else of hers – and I don't have to tell you what it was.

AL: But you admit that you did throw away something?

AD: For the benefit of the tape, Michael Lambert is nodding. Now, Michael, don't you think it would make things easier for all of us if you just told us what it was that you threw away?

ML: I already told you: it's got nothing to do with that bird or her things. I'm not saying any more than that. It's not your business.

AL: If you didn't take the purse, how do you account for it being found next to the path where you ran away, in more or less the same place as witnesses saw you throw this *thing* whatever it was?

ML: That's not for me to say. That's your job. All I know is *I* didn't take it and *I* didn't throw it in them bushes.

AL: It's a bit of a coincidence though, isn't it?

ML: Mmm. Maybe. That's *your* problem though, isn't it? It's nothing to do with me. All I did was to try to help the bleeding bird when she fell over. And this is all the fucking thanks I get!

9 SO FAR, SO GOOD

It looked very much as if Lambert was guilty. And it would have been easy to have charged him with robbery, even if it was unlikely that the assault charge, which the victim was pressing for, would stick. However, there were one or two things that made Anna Davenport cautious about rushing to charge him.

The first thing was Gavin. I think I've told you before that PC Gavin Hughes rather specialised in getting to know the rough sleepers that hung around his patch. He'd come across Lambert before and he reckoned that pinching a woman's wallet while she was lying helpless on the ground was out of character for him – especially considering that, at the time, he appeared to have been unusually sober. Lambert had been in trouble with the police on numerous occasions, but always as a result of drink and never in relation to assault or pickpocketing. In Gavin's opinion, Lambert might not have been above picking up a purse that he found lying around and stealing the cash from it, but he would not have rummaged through Ms Rowland's bag looking for valuables to steal.

Poor Gavin! I think he could see years of patient work building up trust with the homeless community going up in smoke over this one arrest – particularly if it turned out that we'd got it wrong.

The other spanner in the works was the forensic evidence – or rather the lack of it. As you'd expect, the purse was smothered with fingermarks, so it wasn't easy to pick out any of them clearly. The team managed to identify some as belonging to Ms Rowland and they were pretty clear that there were some marks that *weren't* hers. But there were none that could be matched to Lambert's fingerprints. So the only link we had between Lambert and the purse was the location where it was found. In other words, we were assuming that the object that he threw away into the bushes while he was fleeing the scene was the purse that the girls, Katherine and Aimee, found a few minutes later. You might well think that he would hardly have bothered lying about throwing something away if it wasn't the stolen purse, but we knew that the defence counsel would be able to come up with any number of reasons why Lambert might not have wanted to admit to what it was.

Anna instigated a fingertip search of the area around Lambert's flight path. She wanted to be able to confirm in court that every effort had been made to check his story that he had thrown something else, other than the purse, away as he ran. She also wanted to be able to cast doubt on any future claim that he made as to what it really was that he threw away.

Meanwhile, another witness came forward, with a different version of events that changed things completely.

Dr Anastasia Mortlake was a retired Zoology don from Lady Margaret Hall, which is one of the five Women's colleges from the days before they all became co-educational. It's situated at the top end of the University Parks and there's a passage through from the parks to Norham Gardens, which is the road that leads to the main entrance of the college. When she retired, Dr Mortlake moved out of her college rooms and into a flat in one of the old Victorian houses in Fyfield Road, which leads off Norham Gardens on the opposite side from the alleyway from the parks. She suffered from arthritis, but was otherwise very fit for her eighty-four years. She was in the habit of taking a walk in the parks each morning and, whenever the weather was suitable, she would take her lunch with her and eat it sitting on one of the benches there. She had not got involved in the incident between Michael Lambert and Joanne Rowland, but when she saw the reports in the Oxford Times, she contacted the police station and asked to be permitted to give a statement about what she had seen.

When you see the statement, which she insisted on

writing herself, you will see why we had to take it seriously, even though it was not consistent with what the other witnesses had told us. Dr Mortlake had specialised in studying animal behaviour and had been acclaimed for her work on social interaction of South American primates. So she was trained in observing animals in the wild and in recording her observations.

10 STATEMENT BY DR ANASTASIA MORTLAKE, RETIRED FELLOW OF LADY MARGARET HALL, TAKEN BY DS ANNA DAVENPORT

I sat down on my usual bench at about twelve forty-five. I was rather tired because the fine weather had seduced me into walking further than usual. I noticed the man, whose face appeared in the Oxford Times as Michael Lambert, sitting on the next bench along the path, on the opposite side from me. By this, I mean that I was on a bench about fifty yards closer to the Norham Gardens entrance than the one he was sitting on. I recognised his face because I had seen him there often before, but I did not know his name until I read it in the paper. He was sitting alone on the bench reading a tabloid newspaper. I don't remember which one, but it was definitely one of the Red Tops.

I ate my lunch and then I threw the wrappings away in the bin next to the bench where Lambert was sitting. He looked up and saw me, but he didn't say anything. I went back to my bench and got out a book to read. I wanted a rest before starting the walk back.

I was disturbed in my reading by a small dog. It emerged from the bushes at the side of the path opposite me and towards Norham Gardens. It was carrying a large stick, which dragged on the ground as it walked. It walked along the path, passed me and approached the bench where Lambert was sitting. Just then a man, whom I assume must have been its owner, called out from across the grass on the other side of the path. The dog dropped the stick on the path and raced off across the grass.

I watched for a few seconds. Then I was about to go back to my book when I noticed a young woman coming along the path from the direction of the Science Area. She was carrying a smartphone in her left hand and tapping it with her right index finger. I assume she was texting or emailing. I could see that she was not looking where she was going. She caught her right foot on the branch that the dog had left behind and tripped. She tried to right herself, but her high heels made her overbalance and she fell to the ground.

By that time, Lambert had finished his newspaper and was just sitting staring into space. At least that was how it appeared to me. The woman fell down in front of him with her shoulders coming close to his feet. I saw that the newspaper report said that he tripped her up, but that is not possible, because when she fell, she had not yet reached where he was sitting. She fell <u>forward</u> and that is how she came to be in front of him on the ground.

Lambert got down on the ground next to her. I think he was kneeling, but he could have been crouching. He said something that I couldn't hear and he put out his hand towards her. He may have touched her on the shoulder or the arm, I couldn't see distinctly.

The woman shouted out in alarm. She sounded frightened. Two men dressed in jogging kit ran up and started shouting. Then more people came running over, all shouting out. Lambert got himself back up and ran off. The two men ran after him. They all ran right past me and on along the path towards Norham Gardens. I watched them go and then I looked back at the cluster of people around the other bench. The woman was sitting on the bench now and there were about a dozen or more people standing around. One of them must have picked up her handbag because I saw her hand it to her. The first woman took the bag and started rummaging around inside it. Then I saw some of the onlookers getting down on their hands and knees and looking under the bench. One of them – a young man, I think – picked up something that I think was the woman's mobile phone.

Then someone shouted out that the man who had run away had stolen the woman's purse. Several of the other people started running off in the direction that Lambert had gone. I saw them meet the two runners and Lambert, held fast between them. They stopped and talked for a few seconds and then the two joggers brought Lambert back to the bench and some of the others came with them. I noticed two teenaged girls hanging around by the bushes nearby where the two groups met. They disappeared into the bushes when the joggers started dragging Lambert back.

I did not see the policeman arrive. I watched the joggers take Lambert back to the bench and I saw that there was a policeman in uniform standing there, talking to the woman who had fallen over and the crowd that had gathered around her. I assume that he must have come in by the entrance on Parks Road, near to Keble. Two more police officers came running over from that direction a few minutes later.

The two girls came running past me, looking very excited. One of them was carrying something in her hand. They pushed their way through the crowd round the bench. I assume they wanted to speak to the police.

The sun had gone in and it was getting cold sitting outside, so I went home. I did not think that my observations would add anything to what the police already knew. However, when I realised that the man Lambert was being accused of deliberately attacking the woman in order to steal her purse I decided that I ought to tell the police what I saw. I am sure that he did <u>not</u> trip her up – she fell over the branch dropped by the dog. I cannot be certain that he did not take her purse, but I do not think that he had time to do so before he ran off. I am sure that he was not carrying anything in his hand when he ran past me. I did not see the bag until the passer-by handed it to the woman after she had got up on to the bench. I think she may have fallen on top of it and then left it on the ground when she got up, but that is just speculation.

I read in the paper that witnesses saw Lambert throwing the purse away into the bushes as he ran. I did not see him throw anything away, but of course that does not mean that he did not.

*

11 WHAT NEXT?

This was the point at which Anna asked for my advice.

She had about a dozen witnesses whose testimonies were consistent and all pointed towards Michael Lambert having deliberately tripped up Joanne Rowland as she walked past him, and then stolen her purse and subsequently thrown it away for fear of being caught with it on him. Against that, she had PC Gavin Hughes' gut feeling that Lambert was not the sort to assault a woman or even to steal her purse after she had fallen down fortuitously in front of him and dropped her bag, and now the evidence of Dr Anastasia Mortlake, who was adamant that, whatever else Lambert may have done, he did *not* trip up Ms Rowland.

Dr Mortlake's statement had several interesting features. The story of the dog and the branch was entirely new to us and provided the first alternative explanation for Ms Rowland having tripped over. Ms Rowland had given us the impression that her bag had remained over her shoulder throughout the incident, including when she got up and sat down on the bench. Dr Mortlake, however, described it having been left lying on the ground and being picked up by a passer-by. This opened up the possibility that someone other than Lambert could have purloined the purse. Dr Mortlake was the only witness – other than Lambert himself – to have watched the scene unfold from *in front of* Ms Rowland. This meant that she was the only person able to corroborate Lambert's statement that Rowland had been busy with her phone and not looking where she was going.

On the face of it, I was inclined to give more credence to Dr Mortlake's testimony than to that of the other witnesses. She was a trained observer with nothing to gain by lying or embellishing. She had witnessed the incident from close to where the main actions had taken place and she had been sitting in a known location and not running or walking along at an indeterminate pace and unknown distance away. The dog story was new but plausible; there could be no reason for her to make it up and it was unlikely that she could have imagined it.

On the other hand, she was elderly and her sight might not be as good as she believed it to be. She admitted that she was reading a book when the events started unfolding before her, so had she really seen everything that she said she had seen? She had come forward only after she realised that Lambert was accused of assault and robbery, and she came with the stated aim of exonerating him. Was there some unknown link between them that had prompted her to make up a story in his defence?

We sat down together and went through each of the witness statements in turn, noting down similarities and differences and trying to decide which were the most reliable.

Joanne Rowland clearly believed that Lambert had tripped her up – and done it deliberately. However, on re-reading what she had said, I came to the conclusion that, in fact, she had inferred that Lambert had tripped her from having felt something catching her foot and assuming that it must have been Lambert's own foot because she was not aware of anything else being present. We dispatched PC Gavin Hughes and DC Andrew Lepage to search the area around the bench for tree branches, especially any with canine tooth-marks on them!

Ms Rowland clearly also believed that Lambert had got down on the ground beside her with the intention of attacking her. However, it was not clear that she had any evidence for this. She was upset and frightened and Lambert's unkempt appearance and smell of booze did not help to give her confidence that he had her best interests at heart. Moreover, she had evidently been talking with other witnesses before giving her statement and had been told that Lambert was a suspicious character and not to be trusted.

We concluded that there was nothing in Ms Rowland's statement to make us doubt what Dr Mortlake had told us. To double check on this, I interviewed Ms Rowland myself. I didn't find out much from that, but there was one thing that I thought was significant. One thing that counted against the idea that someone else had stolen the purse and thrown it in the bushes was that it seemed pointless to take it and then get rid of it immediately unless it was because the thief was afraid of being caught with it on his person. I pressed Ms Rowland to try to remember exactly what had been in her purse before it was taken from her. Eventually she admitted that she had thought that she had about thirty pounds in notes, as well as the small change that we found in it when it was recovered. She went on to say that she had not said anything about this before because she assumed that she had been mistaken and that she had left the money locked in the desk in her room, where she kept her valuables such as credit cards and passport. I asked her whether she had found the cash when she returned to her room and she admitted that she had not.

Caldwell and Sanders, the two runners, had given statements that were almost identical. This was to be expected, since they had been allowed ample opportunity to compare notes before making them. They neither of them noticed the dog or the stick, but that is not surprising. The dog could have dropped its stick before they came within sight of the bench; or they could simply have not been looking that way when it happened. Caldwell reported having seen Lambert put out his foot to trip Rowland up, but this could easily have been his interpretation of what must have happened after hearing Rowland's own account. The fact that Sanders does not mention what it was that made Rowland fall over supports this theory.

The two schoolgirls, Katie and Aimee, had even longer to discuss together what they had seen. It is greatly to their credit that neither of them said that they saw Lambert throw a purse into the bushes. Instead, they described what he threw as "something small". When I said this to Anna, she told me that she and Monica Philipson had made a particular point of telling the girls before the start of the interview how important it was only to say what they were *sure* they remembered. They'd done this because they were afraid that the girls might allow their imaginations to run wild. I wondered whether perhaps this is something that ought to have been emphasised to the adult witnesses as well.

What Lambert told us in his interview fitted pretty well with what Dr Mortlake said in her statement, but there was something suspicious about his refusal to tell us what he had thrown into the bushes. Fortunately for him – or possibly unfortunately, depending on how you look at it – our team of searchers did eventually find the mysterious object (and a whole lot of other spurious items dropped into the bushes by visitors to the parks over a period of several months by the look of some of them!). Even more lucky for him was the discovery of a large stick – a small branch, one might describe it – with the unmistakable marks of the teeth of a fox terrier impressed upon it. (In case you're wondering: no, our forensics team weren't able to identify the breed solely from the tooth marks. However, those gave them a good idea of the size of dog concerned and an appeal for dog walkers who had been in the parks on the day in question produced the owner of Sam, a fox terrier with a penchant for stick-collecting.)

12 CONCLUSION

And what, I hear you asking, was it that Lambert threw into the bushes? What we found, after hours of patient searching, was a small plastic wallet containing cannabis resin. As soon as we identified the contents, we had our suspicions that this could be what we were looking for. Examination of the outside of the wallet revealed several fingermarks which we managed to match up to Lambert's prints. We were still no further forward as far as finding out who took Ms Rowland's purse (and presumably removed her thirty pounds in notes before discarding it in the bushes) but we did have enough evidence to charge Lambert with possession of an illegal substance.

Reviewing the witness statements again, we came to the conclusion that what must have happened was that one of the onlookers who rushed to Ms Rowland's aid – probably the helpful person who handed her bag to her when she was sitting on the bench after her fall – helped himself, or herself, to the purse and made off with it. Probably he was among those who chased after Lambert when the alarm was raised that the purse had gone missing and he, or she, managed to extract the money while nobody was looking – all eyes were on Lambert, after all. Then, when they heard that Lambert had thrown something in the bushes, they took the opportunity of getting rid of the incriminating purse in a location that would implicate the most likely suspect – probably while pretending to join in the search for the missing item. Finally, they walked away without being noticed, which would have been easy to do since everyone was concentrating on hunting for the purse.

In the end, we let Lambert off with a police caution for possessing cannabis. The quantity was small and almost certainly for his own use. PC Hughes was confident that he was no more than a very minor offender and he was keen to give him the benefit of the doubt. He had already suffered the indignity of being arrested and held overnight in a police cell, which was rather a poor reward for having been the first to offer assistance to Ms Rowland.

We checked and re-checked the fingermarks on the purse against the police database, but we could not find a match. In the end, we called Ms Rowland in to tell her that we were unable to identify who had taken her purse and stolen her thirty pounds. She was very indignant and insisted that it must have been Lambert. I pointed out that he had no time to take the money from the purse and if he had done so, someone would have been bound to see him. Moreover, he had been arrested and searched and no money was found on him. She then reverted to saying that she did not think that there had been any money in the purse.

'In that case,' Anna said, very reasonably, 'you haven't lost anything, so I would try to put the whole incident behind you, if I were you.'

'But he assaulted me! Aren't you going to charge him with that?'

'I'm sorry,' I explained as patiently as I could. 'He says that he was trying to help you up.'

'And you believe him?' she sounded incredulous.

'In the absence of any evidence to the contrary, we have no choice.' I told her. 'We have to treat him as innocent until he is proved guilty.'

She left eventually, still clearly very dissatisfied. I wasn't very pleased with the situation myself. Not because I thought that Lambert was guilty, but because we hadn't been able to find out who had really taken Ms Rowland's purse – and because Ms Rowland and most of the witnesses would all go on believing that they knew exactly who had done it and that the police had let them down by failing to prosecute. But that's police work for you!

ANGIE

(The love of my life.)

1 INTRODUCTION

This is going to be the hardest part of my memoirs to write. In fact, I'm not sure that I'll manage to finish it, but I've decided that I need to try. Looking back, I've written about some of the significant people in my life – Bernie and Jonah have each had their own sections and Lucy has cropped up in a few places – but I haven't done justice to the person who meant – and still means – the most to me. If you've read anything about me at all, you'll know that I'm talking about Angie. She dropped into my life from nowhere as a witness – and at first a potential suspect – in a murder investigation[2] and ended up becoming my wife.

You've probably also heard how our marriage ended twenty-five years later when she was knifed to death on our own kitchen[3]. That, of course, was how I came to be available to marry Bernie and become Lucy's stepfather. In between, there were a lot of years of happy married life, which isn't, I suppose, very exciting to write about. However, I feel obliged to have a go at describing the love of my life. I don't want you to go away thinking that she was an insignificant part of my life – or insignificant compared with Our Bernie, at any rate! And I'm also aware that people sometimes think that I take Bernie for granted and don't seem to appreciate her properly, because I don't pretend to love her the way I loved Angie – and still do.

So here goes! Don't expect a well-crafted story. The beginning and the end you already know, so I'll try to be brief about those, and the middle is going to be a bit of a

---

[2] You can read about how I met Angie in *DC Johns Meets his Match*.

[3] There are accounts of this from Bernie's point of view in *Despise not thy Mother* and *Changing Scenes of Life* (where you can also read how we eventually got to the bottom of who it was who had done it and why).

mish-mash of memories that probably won't mean a lot to anyone except me. I hope it will give you a flavour of the woman that changed my life forever. Nothing I could write could ever give you more than a tiny hint of how wonderful she was or how much I miss her still, but I'll do my best. Just remember that, whatever you think from reading this, she was twice as beautiful and ten times more intelligent and twenty times kinder than I make her sound.

2 JAMAICA 1954 - 1975

Angela Florence Wheeler was born on 25th April 1954 in what was then the Crown Colony of Jamaica. One of her earliest memories was of the independence celebrations in 1962. She was the third of six children born to Sebastian and Victoria Wheeler. The oldest of the family was Christine, who was four years older than Angie. She was closely followed by Meshach and then there was a three-year gap before Angie arrived. Angie had two younger sisters, Phoebe and Sonia, four and eight years younger than her, respectively. I think there may have been another brother or sister between them, who died in childhood, but I'm not sure. And then, there was Joseph – more about him later.

This chapter probably shouldn't really be described as part of my memoirs, because, of course, I wasn't there. The particulars of Angie's childhood and early adulthood in Jamaica are derived from what she told me about it – and the stories that she used to tell our children – and also from talking to Phoebe and Joseph. Joseph spoke movingly at Angie's funeral about their childhood together[4], which was when I fully realised all that she had done for him. I've probably got a lot of the details wrong – I don't know a lot about life in nineteen sixties Jamaica – but the main thrust of the story is correct, and I hope it sets the scene so that you can see what a very special person Angie was.

Angie was very close to her younger sisters, who looked up to her as a role model. Christine seemed to them to be one of the adults, while Angie understood them in a way that nobody else could. Her favourite sibling, however, was her younger brother Joseph. Although Joseph was only two years younger than Angie,

---

[4] You can read about Joseph's speech at Angie's funeral in *Despise not thy Mother*, chapter 16.

she became like a second mother to him because he suffered from cerebral palsy – he was what we called in those days a *spastic*. He had only limited control over his limb movements and was unable to talk. Angie was devoted to him and determined to find a way of helping him to gain more independence. In particular, she was sure that there must be some way of enabling him to speak.

Angie loved helping her mother around the house, and she loved even more helping to look after the younger ones; and most of all, she loved to care for Joseph. She worked out a sort of sign language to enable him to communicate with his family and a few close friends. There was no school that could – or at least, no school that would – take him, so she shared her school books with him and taught him to read. She was very ingenious and managed to rig up a stand for holding a book steady in front of him while he painstakingly worked at persuading his obstinate hands to turn the page.

Of course, since he could not speak, it was impossible to be sure that what he read was what was on the page, but Angie was confident that he understood what he read. Why else would he burst out laughing at the exploits of Winnie-the-Pooh or cry about the fate of Hans Andersen's Little Match Girl?

Angie's family were Methodists and her parents insisted that the children all attend church and Sunday School regularly every week. Angie loved singing the hymns and she was proud when the Sunday School Superintendent presented her with her very own Bible. She kept it in the drawer of the little cabinet that stood on her side of the bed that she shared with Phoebe. This cabinet was the only place that was private from every other member of the family, and it was where she kept all her most precious possessions: the small bamboo plate that someone had given her at her baptism, a china jug that had belonged to her grandmother, a toy rabbit with floppy ears and most of the whiskers worn off, and a small collection of books.

Angie loved playing at school with her younger sisters and Joseph. She would be the teacher and would line them up, sitting on the floor of their yard, while she wrote on the wall of the house with a piece of chalk – always (or almost always) remembering to clean it off again before her father returned home in the evening. He took a dim view of graffiti – even of the improving sort that Angie indulged in.

Angie didn't have a lot of time for playing, though, because she had to help her mother with the household chores – which were all the more because of Joseph's disability. I remember her telling our children about washing by hand – boiling up the clothes in a gigantic pan on the stove, and hanging them out in the yard to dry, and starching the boys' shirts and the girls dresses. Even Joseph used to have a job on washing days: he sat out in the yard keeping watch and ringing a bell if the rain started. Nobody seemed to know where this bell had come from. It was a large, brass instrument fastened to the side of the house, with a long rope dangling down. Joseph was able to hold the rope and ring the bell by pulling hard on it. He was very proud to have such a responsible duty. Angie told me that her father said the bell had once been a ship's bell, but he hadn't been able to explain how it came to be in their family.

Joseph couldn't walk, so his parents – and then later his older brother – carried him everywhere. That was easy when he was small, but as he grew older he became too heavy for his mother to lift easily. Eventually they managed to obtain an old second-hand wheelchair for him. It was too big for him and gave him rather a bumpy ride, but he was delighted with the new mobility that it gave him. Angie loved pushing him around in it. Now she could take him with her when she and Phoebe went out to play on the beach or on the piece of waste ground at the end of their street.

Angie loved to sing. She sang while she worked,

turning the mangle for her mother or holding the pegs while Christine hung up the clothes to dry. She sang the hymns that she learnt at church. One of her favourites (and a favourite with Joseph too) was *This, this is the God we adore*[5]. He remembered this, years later, and we sang it at her funeral.

When Angie was only twelve, she volunteered to help to teach in the Sunday School. Miss Webster, who was in charge of the youngest class, was delighted to have an assistant, and soon Angie was playing at teaching for real. She began to think that she would like to be a teacher when she grew up – and Miss Webster encouraged her in the idea. By that time, her older sister, Christine, was working as a secretary and Meshach was studying hard, with the aim of becoming an engineer. When Miss Webster suggested to Angie's mother that perhaps her daughter had the makings of a teacher, Mrs Wheeler agreed readily with the idea. It would mean Angie going to college, but with three incomes, the family would be able to afford it, and teaching was a respectable and worthwhile career.

But then something happened to change all Angie's plans. Joseph was taken ill with a chest infection, which turned into pneumonia. He was taken into hospital and, for several days, the family feared for his life.

Fourteen-year-old Angie spent a lot of time at Joseph's bedside. She watched and listened and learnt a lot about hospital life – and about human nature. She admired the nurses – most of them – who worked tirelessly to care for their patients. She saw how some of them took time trying to understand Joseph's sign language or asked Angie and her mother to explain it to them. But she also saw that some of them seemed to be embarrassed at Joseph's involuntary movements and grunting attempts at speech.

---

[5] You can find out more about this hymn here:
http://www.singingthefaithplus.org.uk/?p=1147

Some seemed to be trying to avoid being the ones who had to help him out of bed to visit the toilet and some even got angry with him for wetting the bed when he had been unable to attract attention.

One day she overheard one of the nursing assistants talking to the mother of another patient on the ward. The mother looked at Joseph and said, 'it always seems to me that it's a pity that children like that survive. You can't help thinking that it would be kinder to put them out of their misery at birth.'

Angie could hardly believe what she had just heard. What right had this woman to come in and pass judgement on her brother's life like that? What did she know? Didn't she realise what a happy life he led – when he was not languishing in a hospital bed with tubes down his throat? But it got worse.

'Yes. Poor little mite,' the nurse agreed. 'His family are very dedicated to him, but it's hard not to think that maybe it would be better for everyone if he didn't pull through.'

Angie looked at Joseph and held his hand very tight. Didn't they realise that he was listening to them? Did they think he was deaf? More likely, they thought he couldn't understand what they were saying. So many people assumed that, just because he could not talk, Joseph could not understand speech either. But Angie knew that he understood everything.

That was the day that she changed her career plans. Instead of being a teacher, she was going to be a nurse – a good nurse like the ones that she had seen working extra hours to make sure that all their patients were comfortable and well-cared-for – and she was going to see to it that nobody on any ward where she was working would be allowed to talk like that about any of the patients. She was going to make sure that *every* patient was treated just the same, whatever other people thought about their value or the quality of their life.

So, when she left school, Angie went to train as a nurse. It meant going away from home, which was hard for her and harder still for Joseph and her younger sisters. But she came back to visit as often as she could and they all knew that she was working to make things better in the end.

As well as working and studying for her nursing diploma, she tried to find out about ways of helping Joseph to find his voice. She was convinced that there must be some way of helping him to learn to control the muscles in his mouth and throat so that he would be able to make intelligible speech, but it was so difficult to find out what that might be. She discovered that there were people called Speech Therapists, who trained children to speak; but when she approached one of them, they said that Joseph was too old.

In any case, speech therapy was expensive and Angie's family could not afford it. By now, both Christine and Meshach had young families of their own to care for, so the only income was Angie's father's wage and whatever Angie was able to spare from her own meagre student nurse allowance. But she was determined not to give up. She continued to read about Joseph's condition and to speak to doctors and nurses at the hospital where she worked. She became more and more convinced that speech therapy was the answer – if only they could afford to pay for a therapist to give Joseph a trial!

Once she was qualified, Angie renewed her efforts on Joseph's behalf. A therapist from the hospital agreed to visit him at home, in her own time, and assess his problem. She reported that she thought that probably something could be done to help him, but that it would most likely take a long time. He would need many hours of therapy and he would have to work hard in between sessions to practise the skills that they would teach him. She could not afford to do this unpaid, but she would show Angie some exercises that she could teach Joseph to do and, you never knew, maybe once he got started he might manage to teach himself. He was clearly a bright boy.

Angie worked hard to help Joseph – and he worked hard as well – but progress was slow. Angie also taught Phoebe some of the exercises so that she could help Joseph when Angie was not around. After nearly a year of trying, Joseph's speech had improved to the extent that his family could understand a lot of what he was trying to say, but to strangers he still appeared to be talking gibberish. He just couldn't manage to get his voice to make the sounds that he wanted it to. Angie became more and more convinced that he needed professional help.

At the same time, Christine was working on another way of helping Joseph to communicate. She had given him the old second-hand typewriter that she had used to practise her secretarial skills. He found it difficult to use and often got his fingers caught between the keys, but little by little, he started to use it to write short stories and poems. He was very proud indeed when one of his poems was included in the church newsletter.

Angie came to the conclusion that she was never going to be able to save up enough to pay for speech therapy for Joseph from her wages at the hospital in Jamaica. Every time she began to think that she might be getting there, some extra expense would crop up – like when his ancient wheelchair eventually broke beyond repair and the family had to club together to buy a replacement. So, she started looking into ways of increasing her income. Eventually, she decided that the best way to do this would be to go abroad to somewhere where the wages for a qualified nurse would be higher. The obvious option was to go to Britain, which many Jamaicans still viewed as the mother country. She spoke the language and had been born a citizen of a British colony.

So from now on, her savings were directed towards the cost of travelling across the Atlantic to a new home, where she hoped she would be able to earn enough to pay for Joseph's therapy and also to find out about any new treatments for cerebral palsy that there might be. At last, she had enough to pay for an air ticket to London.

Flying was unheard of before in her family. Her grandmother was determined that aeroplanes were the work of the devil and no good would come of them. Her mother was very anxious and kept asking her why she did not go in a Banana Boat, as so many of their friends had done back in the fifties. However, this was 1975 and air travel was becoming cheaper, while the number of boats crossing the Atlantic was diminishing. So, Angie became the first person in her family to fly. Joseph, Phoebe and Sonia were so excited about the prospect that, for a while, they forgot to be sad at losing their favourite sister. The whole family came to the airport to see her off – waving to her as she boarded the plane and set off for a new life on the other side of the world.

3 MIXED MARRIAGE

It must have all seemed a bit bleak for Angie, arriving in England in January 1975. Although January was mild that year, it must have felt cold to someone fresh from the Caribbean. Angie always insisted that the weather did not bother her at all, but it's hard not to suspect that the cold dampness of an Oxford winter must have added to the coldness of the welcome that she experienced in some quarters. She admitted that initially she was disappointed not to have stepped off the aeroplane on to a covering of snow. She had imagined that throughout the winter months the earth was covered with a magical blanket of whiteness, as pictured in the Christmas cards that she had seen, depicting robins on holly twigs and choirboys processing into ancient churches. She did get her wish a few months later. The weather took a chilly turn towards the end of March and she had her first sight of snow in April, when by rights things should have been warming up.

I don't know what brought Angie to Oxford specifically. She had no ties here – but then she knew no-one in England, so anywhere was as good as anywhere else. Perhaps she expected the hospital in a great university city to provide better opportunities than elsewhere for an aspiring nurse. Angie would probably say that it was God's guidance that brought her to Oxford – and she'd probably add that one reason for His choice of destination was to enable her to meet and marry me! In my opinion, if that were the case, it must have been for my sake, not Angie's, because I'm sure He could have found a lot of more promising candidates for her helpmeet than I was. However it happened, she landed up working at the Radcliffe Infirmary and living in the nurses' home.

In those days, a good proportion of the nurses lived in the home, although it was no longer obligatory for them to do so. Angie found herself living as part of a group of six nurses in what amounted to a self-contained flat. I've described the set-up elsewhere, so I won't go into a lot of detail here. Angie always insisted that they were all friendly enough towards her, but there only seemed to be one of them that she really got close to. That was Elaine Gregg. She was a few years older than Angie and had been a staff nurse at the infirmary for five years. She came from somewhere in the West Midlands – Walsall, I think, or it may have been Wolverhampton – and spoke with a strong Black Country accent. Like Angie, she came from a large family and she loved to talk about the doings of her brothers and sisters, who used to visit her at the home from time to time. Elaine was the oldest of a string of children. I could never keep track of them – it seemed as if there must have been at least a dozen, but perhaps that was just me getting confused.

Angie became a sort of adopted aunt to the younger Greggs, who loved to listen to her stories of life in Jamaica. I remember Angie getting particularly fond of the youngest girl, Tracey, who reminded her of her own youngest sister Sonia. Tracey was nearly twenty years younger than Elaine. I think she was eight or nine when Angie first met her. I remember being introduced one day, when I visited Angie at the nurses' home. They had been baking together and Tracey was very proud of her Jamaican patties.

As you may have read elsewhere,[6] Angie and I became acquainted during the course of my first murder investigation as a Detective Constable. Susan Parry, the nurse who occupied the room next to hers, was found dead in her room one evening. The police were called when it turned out that she had been stabbed in the heart.

[6] Chapter 12 of *Despise Not thy Mother* is Angie's version of our first meeting, as she told it in her contribution to Lucy's book about her father, DS Richard Paige. I've also written about it in one of my earlier memoirs, *DC Johns Meets his Match*.

I won't bore you with the details, but the upshot was that another nurse from the group of six was eventually charged with her murder, leaving just four of the original set sharing the flat. A short while afterwards they were joined by two newly-qualified nurses, twins who kept themselves very much to themselves. So Angie's only real friend was still Elaine Gregg.

Outside of the hospital and nurses' home, Angie found companionship through joining one of the local Methodist churches. They were delighted when they discovered that she had taught in the Sunday School in her home church, and soon she had joined the staff of the "Junior Church". I may be misjudging them, but I rather fancy that they were quite proud to have a black teacher among their number. It showed off how broadminded they were and they probably thought that it would broaden the minds of the children as well.

It was indirectly through her involvement in the Junior Church that I got to know Angie better. As I'm sure I've mentioned before, I was brought up by the National Children's Home. (It changed its name to *NCH Action for Children* and then to just *Action for Children*[7], after it switched from running homes for orphaned and abandoned children to more general ways of helping disadvantaged kids.) Back in those days, there used to be an annual fund-raiser, where Sunday Schools and Brownie packs used to "sell" photographs of children from the home[8] to their friends and neighbours. Then, in each district, there would be an event where the cash raised was

---

[7] See https://www.actionforchildren.org.uk/.

[8] It's hard to imagine this happening now. We would be accused of exploiting the children and exposing them to danger of harm but, at the time, we thought nothing of it. I was never chosen to have my photograph included in the *Sunny Smiles* booklet – I don't think I was photogenic enough – but I would never have minded if I had been.

handed over. This was called the *Festival of Queens,* because each group would dress up one of their little girls as a queen and they would parade up the aisle on to the stage, accompanied by one or two maids of honour.

I went along to support the cause, because I was always grateful to the Home for having given me a good start in life. Angie was there with her Sunday School class. She had also had a hand in making the costumes, which seemed to me, at any rate, to be among the best there. By pure coincidence, we ended up sitting next to each other.

I tried, not very successfully, to make small talk with her. During our conversation, she let slip that there were people in the hospital who were suggesting that *she* was the most likely suspect in the murder of Nurse Parry, purely because she was black and from the West Indies. I'm afraid I reacted rather badly to that and probably embarrassed Angie dreadfully.

My "family" in the home had included children from all sorts of racial backgrounds and we'd all had it drummed into us pretty hard that everyone was the same underneath. Any sort of teasing or bullying on racial grounds would have been treated as the worst possible offence. I remember vividly a preacher at church telling us that God was colour blind when it came to people – and that we ought to be too. In the current climate of *valuing diversity*, I suspect he would have been condemned for suggesting that race and ethnic background are an irrelevance. Nowadays we would have been encouraged to see God's work in the rich tapestry of different cultures and to celebrate the variety. However, I digress.

The good thing about my getting hot under the collar when I heard about this contemptible slur on Angie's character, was that she agreed to come outside with me to talk properly. And the upshot of that was that we went for a lovely long walk in Christ Church Meadow and only went back to the town hall when it was time for Angie to escort her Sunday School class home. She told me about her family back in Jamaica – and especially about Joseph and how much she hoped that the money that she was able to send back home was helping him. I even plucked up the courage to ask her for a tentative date at some unspecified time in the future.

Of course, it would have been most improper for us to go out together while Angie was still a witness – and indeed a suspect – in a police investigation; so I had to bide my time and wait until it was over to realise my dream. Fortunately, we had an unexpected breakthrough only a week or so later and I was put out of my misery. I don't know what would have happened if this had turned into one of the many unsolved cases that are left open for years. I suppose that eventually I would have stopped being actively involved and our relationship would have been permitted, but it would always have been a very awkward situation.

As I mentioned before, the culprit turned out to be another of Angie's flatmates – Sister Catherine Spencer – who had killed Susan Parry to prevent her from revealing that she had been pilfering diamorphine from the ward stock. From my point of view, the main thing was that I was now free to ask Angie out.

It sounds rather corny, but our first date was the Police Dance. I'd been getting ragged for weeks because I wouldn't say whom I was bringing with me. (Actually, I'd been planning not to go, but saying that outright would have provoked more comments, quite possibly including questions being mooted about my sexual orientation. The Police Service was still a rather *blokey* place to be in those days.) So, inviting Angie to accompany me killed two birds with one stone from my point of view.

I'm not a great dancer, but Angie is very patient and forbearing and she very kindly refrained from commenting on the way I kept missing the steps and getting my feet tangled. At least I managed to avoid stepping on her toes! By about halfway through the evening I was quite convinced that she was the only woman for me.

There was a very nasty incident towards the end, which could have landed me in a lot of bother if my boss, DI Richard Paige, hadn't been there to take charge. PC Mark Adams was standing by the bar with a group of his cronies. They'd all had a few by then and he was getting unsteady on his feet. He lurched into Angie and spilled his drink all down her dress. Then he had the gall to accuse *her* of causing the accident and he used some quite outrageous racially abusive language towards her. I saw red and was on the verge of punching him on the nose – not that I knew how, but I was so angry I was willing to give it a go – when Richard stepped in between us. He ordered me to take Angie outside and then gave Adams a public dressing down. I wouldn't have liked to have been in Adams' shoes, I can tell you!

I walked Angie home and we arranged to go to the pictures together a few days later. I won't bore you with a ball-by-ball commentary on our courtship, but suffice it to say that we saw a good deal of on another over the next few months. Angie's flatmates seemed very accepting of my presence in their communal kitchen whenever Angie entertained me to dinner, and the members of her church welcomed me with open arms. (I think they had in mind all the jobs that a young man might be persuaded to take on once he became a fully-paid-up member. However, I was able to explain that my erratic working hours made it impossible for me to undertake the role of scoutmaster or property steward.)

I suppose this might be a good point at which to offer some sort of explanation of my relationship with the church. Lucy always says that I don't believe in God, but it's not quite as simple as that sounds. I was taken to Methodist church services when I was a child and I grew up accepting the idea of some sort of God-force behind the creation of the universe. Because of my upbringing, going to church always seemed to be the obvious thing to do on Sunday mornings. However, when I joined the police, I often had to work at weekends, and that broke the routine of church attendance. Moreover, moving to Oxford meant that I didn't have a church that was *mine* so to speak. So, until I met Angie, I'd rather given up on religion, and it didn't seem to have made a lot of difference to my life doing so.

Being thrown in with a new crowd of colleagues also brought into question the beliefs that I'd previously accepted without really thinking about them. For the first time in my life, I came across people who thought the whole idea of belief in God was comical. I also got some flak over having been brought up in a children's home – except that my tormentors chose to call it an orphanage – so I kept my head down and didn't admit to having been a church member. I was very busy swotting for my police exams and setting up home for myself for the first time; churchgoing wasn't high up on my agenda.

Meeting Angie changed all that. For her, church was the centre of her life – ranking in importance marginally ahead of her job and neck-and-neck with her family – and she naturally assumed that I would share her enthusiasm. For a while, she swept me along – or perhaps more accurately, I was swept along by my devotion to her – and I even began to think that I really did believe in the sort of personal saviour God that she was so certain of. I'm quite sure that I meant it, a couple of years later, when I joined in with the *amen* after the minister called for God's blessing on our marriage – but I'm getting ahead of myself.

It's probably a deficiency on my part, but I've never felt the sorts of things that other people talk about when they talk about God. I've never *felt my heart strangely warmed*, like John Wesley or *known Jesus Christ as my personal saviour* as so many of the evangelical preachers put it. I've certainly never had any sort of Damascus road experience. I'm a pretty down-to-earth sort of guy and it always seems to me that the chances are there's nothing else beyond what we can see and hear and feel with our hands. But I'd rather like it if I were proved wrong.

I still like the friendship that I find in the church and I still enjoy singing the hymns, although I sometimes feel hypocritical because I'm not sure that I subscribe to a lot of the sentiments expressed in them. Singing the hymns that Angie loved makes me feel closer to her than anything else does – and I wish that I could believe that this is because she's alive somewhere and waiting for me to join her – but I know the psychologists would explain that easily by talking about past associations in my own mind. Anyway, that's quite enough of me and my personal hang-ups; this story is supposed to be about Angie.

We'd been going out together for about six months, I suppose, when we started talking about marriage. But we didn't feel able to become formally engaged because our financial circumstances made it seem like an impossible dream. A detective constable's salary was meagre and I knew that Angie would not be happy if she could not continue to send a good part of her own wages home to her family in Jamaica. In those days, it was still accepted practice that women would give up work, or at least reduce their hours considerably, if they had children, so I felt that I ought to get to a point where I could support us both – and contribute to Angie's family – before we tied the knot.

Fortunately for me, Richard seemed to like the way I worked and wanted me to progress. He pushed me to take my sergeant's exams and supported my application for promotion. My detective sergeant's salary was just sufficient to enable us to get a mortgage on a small terraced house in East Oxford, not far from Angie's church. It needed quite a bit of work doing on it, but I could manage that – and some of her friends from church gave us a helping hand in lieu of a wedding present. Most of our combined savings went on the deposit, so we had to start saving all over again for the honeymoon, which we were determined was to be in Jamaica. Angie's family could not afford to come over to attend the wedding, so we wanted to visit them right away afterwards. She said that she wanted to show me off – I wasn't convinced that they would be impressed with her catch!

Predictably, there was quite a lot of friendly – and not-so-friendly – banter at work when I announced my matrimonial plans. Adams in particular made some very crude remarks and even a few of the officers that I regarded as friends seemed a bit taken aback at the idea of my actually *marrying* a black woman. One even took me to one side and asked point blank whether it was a shotgun wedding and suggested that I should not allow myself to be pressurised into doing something that I might regret later.

People from church all seemed delighted at the match and they were falling over themselves to help. I suppose they had probably heard the same sorts of sermons about God's colour blindness as I had.

The one big surprise for both of us was Elaine Gregg's reaction. She had always been very friendly towards me and had never said a word against our going out together; but when Angie told her that we were going to get married, she looked first shocked, then disapproving and finally upset. Angie didn't know how to interpret this or how to reassure her friend that all was well. She wondered if Elaine was in some way jealous of me, so she tried to make her see that their friendship wouldn't change. She talked about how they would still be working together afterwards, even though they would not be living together in the nurses' home any more. She talked about our wedding plans and asked Elaine to be her chief bridesmaid. Elaine looked horrified at the idea.

'I really appreciate you asking me,' she said, after a long pause, 'but really, I couldn't. It would be hypocritical of me, when I really do think you're making a big mistake marrying Peter. Not that I've got anything against Peter,' she added hastily, 'but I've seen mixed marriages back home and they never work out. It's not fair on the kids – being neither one thing nor the other.'

Angie was really upset by her friend's reaction, but luckily for me, she didn't accept her arguments. To be fair to Elaine, she didn't say anything more after that outburst. She'd stated her case and then left us to it. She even came along to the wedding service, with some of the other nurses, and behaved impeccably, pretending to be pleased for us. But she and Angie could never be the close friends that they had been before.

Richard had been so instrumental in bringing us together that he was the obvious candidate for Best Man. Angie had a whole string of little bridesmaids – all the girls in her Sunday School class – with one of the other teachers as chief bridesmaid. People sometimes comment that our wedding photographs look rather odd, with so many little girls clustering around the bride. They usually go on to say how sweet it is to see them all. I think that often what they really mean is that it's strange that Angie's is the only black face among so many white ones, but they are too polite to put that into words.

We were on a strict budget, so Angie made her own dress, I wore my best suit and all the bridesmaids simply wore their best dresses. The cake was also home-made – a present from another of Angie's many friends.

Everything went off wonderfully well. I think I can truly say that it was the happiest day of both our lives, so far – up until a few moments before we left for the airport for our flight to Kingston. I was waiting outside for the car to come to drive us to the station, while Angie was changing into her going away outfit. The wedding guests were all standing expectantly in a cluster behind me waiting to wave us goodbye. Everyone was chattering away and I wasn't really listening to the various conversations that were going on, but unaccountably I overheard a brief exchange between two of the older members of the church congregation.

'They make a lovely couple, don't they?'

'Well, you may say that, but think of the poor children!'

4 THE KIDS

'Think of the Poor children!'

Those words haunted me for years afterwards. However, it was not until about eighteen months after our marriage that any 'poor children' showed signs of being on their way. We hadn't been confident of embarking on parenthood until we were sure that we could afford such things as food, clothing and the mortgage. However, as we neared the end of 1979, we decided to take the plunge.

It happened far quicker than we had expected. In the beginning, we didn't realise what it was. I was convinced that there must be something seriously wrong with Angie. At first, we thought it must be food poisoning, but after more than a week of sickness, we realised that it must be more than that, and I feared the worst. It never occurred to us that it could be morning sickness, because it lasted all day – and even got her up in the night on a few occasions. You can imagine how surprised and delighted we were when our GP suggested a pregnancy test.

As the weeks wore on, however, and Angie seemed no better, I started to feel quite guilty for what she was going through, and privately vowed that one baby was quite enough and I would insist that we remained as a family of three. I also felt guilty that Angie was so far from home at a time when she might quite reasonably want the support of her mother. With her usual good nature and optimistic outlook, she pooh-poohed all my misgivings and declared herself quite content with her lot.

Nonetheless, I was very relieved when the sickness eased off in the second trimester and Angie appeared the picture of good health. It did not seem long, however before the heat of the summer started to take its toll and, as she entered the final weeks of pregnancy, Angie was very tired and languid. I well remember those long, hot August nights when she would be lying next to me in bed, fidgeting in an attempt to get comfortable, while at the same time trying not to disturb me. To make matters worse, Hannah arrived nearly two weeks late, extending the long wait. During that time, we were very grateful for Bernie, who came in most days, while I was out at work, to help with the housework so that Angie could put her feet up.

Knowing no better, I always assumed that the swollen ankles and exhaustion that Angie endured in those last two months before Hannah finally made her debut were the inevitable consequences of pregnancy. It came as quite a shock to me when Bernie was expecting, to find her still as energetic as ever, right up to the day of Lucy's birth. She claims never to have experienced the slightest hint of morning sickness either. It just goes to show that everyone is different and you can never know how someone else will react to any situation.

Hannah finally made her entrance into the world in the early hours of a Monday morning, which was quite convenient, since it meant that I could be there at the birth and still go into work that day. (I'm not sure how much use I was, what with being tired out from being up all night and with my mind very much on other things than policing!) Hannah was, and is, very beautiful. She inherited Angie's lovely almond-shaped dark brown eyes and high cheek bones. Her skin was a gorgeous caramel shade, which darkened as she got older, but remains paler than Angie's delightful rich chocolate complexion. It always goes darker in the sunshine too, which surprises a lot of people. As far as I can make out, that is my sole contribution to my daughter's looks – but then she's better off without my inflammatory red hair and troublesome pale skin.

Although we might have liked Angie to give up work and become a full-time mum, the state of our family finances simply wouldn't allow it. Maternity leave and maternity pay was less generous then and there was no right for those with caring responsibilities to request part-time or flexible working. However, with us both working shifts, we did manage to arrange things so that we could share the job of looking after Hannah and reduce the amount of childcare that we needed. Once more, I realised how much we were losing out by being so far away from Angie's family. While friends and colleagues with young children relied on grandparents to look after them while they were at work, we either had to pay or to fall back on our friends. Some of the women that Angie had met at the antenatal classes were willing to help out, but mostly we relied on Bernie to fill in the gaps.

Looking back, I'm surprised how little I saw of Bernie in those days. I know that she put in far more hours than was reasonable, covering the times between Angie setting off for her shift and me getting home from mine, or vice versa, but she always hurried off as soon as I arrived, as if she didn't want to be in the house with me unless Angie was there too. I suppose she didn't want to intrude or come between me and my daughter. Whatever the reason, she remained very much Angie's friend and not mine, and I didn't really get to know her.

Luckily for us, Hannah was a very placid baby – she came into her own in the *driving-her-parents-up-the-wall* stakes as a teenager – and we started to think that parenthood was basically very easy. We didn't have nearly as many sleepless nights as most parents seem to complain of – which was just as well seeing as our jobs both often required us to be up early and always demanded our full attention.

I loved the times when I was off duty and could spend the whole day playing with Hannah or taking her out. I even enjoyed shopping, which had never before been one of my favourite activities. Wherever we went and whatever we were doing, she found something to get excited about – whether it was a big yellow digger mending the road or a sparrow picking up crumbs.

I did get some funny looks sometimes, though.

Sometimes it was comical and sometimes annoying and sometimes I was hard-pressed to keep my temper. In those days, it was still fairly unusual for a man to have responsibility for a young child – dads mostly only got involved when their offspring were old enough to go with them to the match or learn to ride a bike. So that was another reason why Hannah and I got stares when I took her out with me in her pushchair or fed her when we were out for the day or – most unexpected of all – changed her nappy!

Young mothers, especially, often congratulated me on my efforts – with a tone in their voices that suggested that they were surprised that a mere man could cope with something as difficult as spooning baby food into an infant's mouth. That wasn't too bad and I tried not to let it irritate me. What was much worse were the people who assumed that Hannah was adopted and congratulated me on my generosity in taking on someone else's offspring. It never seemed to occur to them that Hannah might be my own daughter.

Worst of all were the people who went on to say how much they admired me for being prepared to adopt a *black* child – as if that made Hannah less desirable. Usually, if I explained the real state of affairs to them, they looked suitably embarrassed and apologised. But there were those who looked disapproving and even a few who said openly that they thought I had made a mistake in entering a mixed-race marriage. They always *said* that it was because the children were bound to suffer through being neither one thing nor the other, but I always wondered if they really meant that they didn't approve of white people mixing with other races.

I think things have improved a lot now. I certainly hope so.

I ought to add that disapproval of mixed-race marriages wasn't confined to the white community. I didn't get any flak from black people at that stage – probably because there weren't as many black families around in Oxford as white ones – but as I'll explain later, it was black disapproval of Angie marrying a policeman that turned out (literally) to be the real killer. But I'm getting ahead of myself. I was telling you about life as a young couple with their first baby.

Although I loved Hannah to bits and enjoyed every minute of the time I spent with her, after the traumatic hours of labour, I was even more determined than before that one child was quite enough. However, Angie had other ideas. Since my main objections to a larger family were to spare her the discomfort, pain and risk, I found it difficult to argue with her clear desire for another baby. Thus it was that, almost exactly two years after Hannah's arrival, our son, Edward, was born.

We'd been hoping for a spring baby – at least that had been my plan, mindful of Angie's discomfort during the hot summer months leading up to Hannah's arrival – but in the event it took Angie several months to conceive and so she had to go through the whole hot and tiring ordeal again. And once again we were very grateful for Bernie and some of Angie's other friends for helping out.

Now that we had Eddie, we suddenly started to realise how lucky we had been with Hannah, who, we now recognised, had been an exceptionally placid and well-adjusted baby. Eddie soon saw to it that we had enough sleepless nights to bring us up to the normal average for young parents. At the same time, Hannah was going through the *terrible twos* and would throw tantrums completely at random. Well, I say *at random* but it always seemed as if she waited to pick the most embarrassing possible moments, or else the times when we were in the greatest hurry and could not afford to spend time arguing with or cajoling her.

Of course, we got through it somehow. Angie was a wonderful mum. She'd had some practice, I suppose, helping to bring up her younger sisters and brother, but I think it was mainly her good nature and unfailing patience that was most important. I did my best, but maybe it's always harder for a dad to get close to his kids, or maybe I didn't try hard enough. Looking back, I realise that I could have made a bigger effort not to let the job get in the way of family life, but I was always nervous of asking for time off unless I absolutely had to. And, of course, my boss didn't have any family, so naturally he didn't think to suggest it.

I don't know whether I managed to get to more of Hannah's sports days and school concerts and things, or whether it always seemed worse when I let Eddie down because he was a boy and wanted his dad to be involved more than Hannah did; but it certainly felt to me as if I kept on making promises to him and then not keeping them. It must have felt like that to him too, because that's what he thought about when he wrote a piece for Bernie's book of memories about Richard[9]. He wrote about the time that Bernie managed to get FA cup final tickets for the three of us to go to Wembley, and I pulled out because Richard called me into work at the last minute; and he went on to describe his disappointment that I missed seeing him win his race at the school sports day a few weeks later. What I didn't know about until Eddie wrote it down, was Richard meeting him from school after that and apologising. I suppose that means I must have complained to him about it, although I don't remember doing so.

I suppose my never spending enough time with Eddie may have been one of the factors that contributed to the problems that we had with him after he transferred to secondary school. I think there was bullying too, but he never spoke about it to Angie or me[10]. We only realised

---

[9] See *Despise not thy Mother*, chapter 13.

[10] Actually, I found out much, much later, that he did tell Angie that there had been some boys making racist remarks,

that there was anything wrong when the school called us in to tell us about his truancy. I was mortified! A policeman's kids ought to know how to behave. And I couldn't understand why Eddie had done it – or, more to the point, why he hadn't told us that he was unhappy at school.

Angie and I both tried reasoning with him, but he just wouldn't talk. We decided that we'd have to accompany him to the school gates every morning to make sure that he got there. That was easier said than done, but we managed to organise our shifts so that we could do it. His school attendance improved, but he took to going off after school and hanging round street corners with some of his mates; so we started waiting for him after school and walking him home as well.

Then we discovered that he was bunking off at lunch time; so we tried to arrange to meet him and bring him home for lunch as well. All the time, we knew that keeping him more and more under our thumbs wasn't the answer, but we really didn't know what else to do.

We were at our wits' end. As children, neither of us had ever felt any reluctance to go to school and we didn't understand why Eddie did. I was worried that it might be something to do with being one of very few black children in a predominantly white school, but Eddie always fiercely denied it if I raised the question of teasing or bullying. Angie tried talking to him about it too, but he insisted that had nothing to do with it. It was just that school was boring, he told us.

Bernie helped out when we couldn't organise our working patterns around getting Eddie to and from school. He seemed to find it easier to talk to her. Maybe this was because she knew more about some of the things that he was interested in – computers, for instance. In those days, home computers were just starting to become, not

but he swore her to secrecy because he was afraid that if I got to hear about it I'd go off the deep end and cause a scene.

common exactly, but more accepted than they had been. In other words, it was no longer only a few nerds who had them. Eddie had asked for one for his birthday, but we weren't keen on him having something that we didn't really understand – not to mention the price, which was way more than we usually spent on the kids for their birthdays!

I don't know whether Eddie complained about it to Bernie or if she just got talking with him about his interest in computers. However it happened, she realised that this was something that she could turn to our advantage by giving Eddie something positive to do with his spare time and showing him how important attending school and getting through his exams was going to be if he wanted to continue to pursue his interest.

She got hold of a second-hand computer for him, from the university. I don't know whether it cost her anything. She made out that it was being thrown out and she was doing them a favour taking it away, but that may just have been to make us feel better about accepting it. I remember her bringing it round one evening and setting it up in his bedroom. We didn't see either of them for the rest of the day. I was very sceptical about it all at the time, but at least now he was staying at home instead of wandering the streets and perhaps getting into trouble with gangs and drugs.

To cut a long story short, Bernie managed to convince Eddie that he had a future in the computer business – but only if he knuckled down and got some decent GCSEs and then A' levels and a Computer Science degree. We'd been telling him how important his education was for years, but of course he wasn't going to listen to us – we were only his parents, after all! Bernie could speak with more authority because she was in the higher education game herself and was able to tell him about the sorts of things that her students had gone on to do after leaving university. She could also tell him how difficult it was going to be for him to get a decent job if he failed all his exams!

Looking back at what I've just written, I seem to be getting a bit off track with this chapter, which was supposed to be all about what a great mother Angie was. Some of what I've just been talking about ought to have gone in the piece I wrote about Our Bernie. And maybe I should have written separate sections for each of the kids. Or perhaps they could have written about what Angie was like as a mother better than I can. Just take it from me – she was good at it, really good. And I know that the kids would agree with me on that.

Now, where was I?

Hannah decided to follow her mother into nursing. We were both delighted about that. Hannah has a naturally empathetic disposition, which makes her ideal for reassuring nervous patients. From a purely practical point of view, nursing is also one of the safest careers to choose – there are never enough nurses to go round! I was taken aback, and a bit disappointed when she decided to go away to train. Angie, however, pointed out that it was understandable that she wouldn't want to be working at the same hospital as her mother. I think I can understand that, but I didn't see why she had to go all the way up to Leeds. There were plenty of places much closer to Oxford that she could have chosen.

I was even more disappointed when she got her first job up there and appeared all set to make her permanent home 175 miles away from us. Once again, Angie seemed to understand, but I was quite at a loss. I wanted her back close to us, and I felt rather hurt that she didn't seem to want us as much as we wanted her. I've never had any parents, so I suppose I'm in no position to pass judgement. Maybe I'd have felt the same in her position.

After a while, we became aware that she had a

boyfriend. She didn't tell us about it right away – I expect she was afraid we'd make too much of a big thing of it, or maybe she wanted to wait until she was sure it was going to last before she introduced him to us. Whatever the reason it did create a rather funny situation.[11] Laurence got to know that she hadn't told us about him and he jumped to the conclusion that it must be because he was white. You see, he hadn't realised that Hannah's parents weren't both black; so he imagined that we might be worried about her embarking on a mixed-race relationship. We all laughed rather a lot when we found out about it. Luckily, Laurence could also see the funny side and didn't get offended.

Laurence is a paramedic. Hannah met him during the course of her work. I'm not sure how he washed up in Leeds. He comes from Walsall, or is it Wolverhampton – somewhere in the West Midlands, anyhow. No! I remember now – it's Wednesbury. I think it's quite racially-mixed there, so he didn't think twice about asking Hannah out, but he must have known that not all parents are overjoyed at the idea of their kids marrying out of their own community.

One of the enduring sadnesses of my life – and Hannah's too, I think – is that Angie didn't live to see them married or to see her grandchildren. Bernie says that she's still watching over us, but I just can't have that sort of confidence. It seems much more likely to me that life on Earth is all there is and there isn't anything beyond the grave. In any case, however wonderful heaven – or whatever you like to call it – might be; to be up there, looking down and seeing little Emily and Amber can't possibly compare with holding them in your arms and seeing their perfect little fingers grasping one of yours, or hearing them trying to say *granddad*, or catching them as

---

[11] You can read all about it in chapter 15 of *Two Little Dickie Birds*.

they toddle towards you for the first time.

I try not to have favourites, but I have to admit to a soft spot for Emily, Hannah's firstborn. This is because she is the only member of the family to have inherited my red hair. Lucy tells me that there must be red hair on Laurence's side of the family too, but he isn't aware of any. Apparently, the genes can get passed down for generation after generation and then red hair appears unexpectedly when a baby inherits it from both sides.

Now it's Hannah's turn to be the odd-one-out in her family and to get the surprised stares and enquiries from strangers as to whether her children are adopted. Amber is darker than Emily, but she still looks white, rather than black, and her hair is a lovely warm brown colour – darker than her dad's but not much darker. Hannah's also having to learn about keeping redheads out of the sun to stop them burning – just as I had to find out about managing afro-style hair and dry skin. Laurence is very laid-back about everything and seems to rejoice in the challenges. He likes to describe it as *the rich tapestry of life*!

Eddie emigrated to Jamaica after his mum died. I'll talk more about that in the next chapter. He's married to a Jamaican nurse called Crystal. So you can see how both of the kids wanted to keep up the nursing tradition that Angie started. It was a long time before they had any children. In fact, I think they were starting to think that it wasn't going to happen for them. However, after seven years, they now have a little boy. Bernie was very touched that they chose to call him Richard, after her Richard. It shows that Eddie must have forgiven him in the end for keeping me at work when I should have been watching him win races or play in the school band.

5 Death, Judgement and Future Life

I chose the title *Death, Judgement and Future Life* for this last section of my memories of Angie, for two reasons: firstly it's the title of a section in the 1933 Methodist Hymn Book, which I became familiar with as a child in the National Children's home and which was the current hymn book in Angie's church in Oxford when we first met; and secondly, it sums up what happened when I lost Angie. She died (obviously) and there was judgement (eventually) for the people who killed her, and life went on (albeit changed for ever) for me and Hannah and Eddie and everyone else who knew Angie. In the current hymnbook[12], the corresponding section is called Death, Judgement and *Eternal* Life. I'm not so sure about that. I'd love to believe that one day I'll be reunited with Angie and we'll be together forever, but … well, I've never seen anything yet that convinced me it's more than wishful thinking.

We'd been married for nearly twenty-five years when it happened. Like the typical husband that I was, I'd completely forgotten that our silver wedding was coming up. I got ready to go out as normal and kissed Angie goodbye on the doorstep. She was off-duty that day and I remember asking her if she had anything planned. She said something vague about needing to do some shopping. Then I went off and that was that.

What Angie didn't tell me was that she had arranged for Bernie to drive her over to Abingdon to get me something for our silver wedding. I don't know why we went there before we got married, instead of buying our rings in Oxford, but we did, and Angie had decided to go to the same jeweller to find me something special for the occasion. I suppose it was a bit of nostalgia for her to be

---

[12] *Singing the Faith*, © Trustees of the Methodist Church, 2011.

going back there after all those years. I don't know what she expected to find – you can't really buy jewellery for a man the way you can for a woman. Anyway, I never found out, because she didn't get there.

I can still see the scene in my mind's eye of me sitting at my desk that morning, trying to decide which piece of mindless paperwork to tackle first, when the Chief Super walked in. That was unheard of and my immediate reaction was to try to think what it was that I could have done wrong to warrant him coming to give me a dressing-down in person. Then I saw his face, and I suddenly knew that he had come to break some bad news. He had that look that policemen put on when they go round to see the family of a victim of violent crime or of a traffic accident.

He told me that Bernie had rung him and asked him to tell me that Angie was dead. Of course, he didn't put it in quite those blunt terms. I'm sure he let me down very gently, but I can't remember the words at all – only the dreadful pounding of my heart as I tried to take it all in. Of course, I wanted to go over right away and see for myself. A uniformed officer drove me – I don't remember her name – and we parked a few doors down, because there were so many vehicles outside already, what with the ambulance and police cars and Bernie's car as well. It seemed to take forever to get there and all the time I was wondering what Bernie was doing there that morning.

The next thing I remember was standing there in the kitchen, looking down on Angie's body. She had on a pale-coloured summer dress, with flowers on. It had red patches all over it where the blood had oozed from multiple stab wounds. I'd seen plenty of dead bodies before – some in even worse condition than Angie's was – but it's all different when it's someone you know. I don't know how long I stood there staring, before someone took me by the arm and led me back outside.

The first thing I saw then was Bernie talking to DCI Gordon MacBride. The Chief Super had put him in charge of the investigation into Angie's murder. And then, the next thing I knew, there was little Lucy grabbing me round the legs and frantically asking to be picked up. My first thought was that she must have been inside and seen the horrors in the kitchen, so I was relieved when Bernie explained that she'd left Lucy in the car while she went to let Angie know that they were there. Nevertheless, it must have been deeply traumatic for a three-year old to see all the grown-ups running round like headless chickens trying to work out what had happened.

Bernie insisted on taking me home with them – and MacBride insisted that we were driven by DI Alison Brown. On the way there, we discovered that Lucy had been taking in more than we thought, when she asked, very straightforwardly if Angie was dead. Bernie, being Bernie, answered her in a similarly straightforward way, which clearly surprised Alison. I wasn't surprised, because I knew Our Bernie, but I did wonder whether it was wise being quite so open with a child as young as that. Lucy doesn't seem to have come to any harm from it, so I suppose her mother probably knew best.

MacBride came round in the afternoon and questioned us both. It was only then that I realised that Bernie and I must both be under suspicion – me of having killed Angie before I went to work and Bernie of having done it when she got to the house. It was during the police questioning that Bernie told me about the business of going to Abingdon to get a wedding anniversary present for me. I know it's illogical, but it somehow made me feel guilty, as if I was responsible for Angie's death. It just seemed so awful that she had been thinking of me and planning a surprise present for me and I thought that, if she hadn't been waiting for Bernie to take her to Abingdon, she'd probably have gone out by then, to do the weekly shop. Years later, Bernie told me that she had blamed herself for arriving just too late to stop it. Apparently she actually heard the killers in the house, but they'd gone by the time she'd opened the door. I don't know what that says about us both. The psychologists probably have a name for it – some sort of syndrome, I expect.

After MacBride had gone, I suddenly realised that I had to break the news to Hannah and Eddie – not to mention informing Angie's employer and her family in Jamaica and her friends at church. It was awful telling the kids over the phone, but there really wasn't any alternative. Hannah and Laurence insisted on driving down to Oxford that very night, despite my trying to persuade them that they were in no fit state. They arrived safely enough, so probably I was worrying unnecessarily and they knew what they were doing. Eddie came down on an early morning train the following day. We all stayed with Bernie, because our house was still cordoned off by the police as a crime scene.

I won't describe the police investigation. I wasn't in any mood to pay a lot of attention and, as the days and weeks and eventually months wore on, I started to accept that we were never going to find out who it was that was responsible. In my job, I've often had to admit to crime victims that we've failed, and to try to explain to them why we can't continue to investigate their case actively any longer. It wasn't until it happened to me that I really understood how unsatisfactory that was for them. I'd always been a bit scathing of the people who demand "closure", as if knowing who had injured them – and presumably, knowing that they were being punished – somehow made things better for them. Now, I started to see things from their point of view.

It wasn't that I wanted revenge. I just wanted to be able to stop looking at all my neighbours – especially my white neighbours, because we all assumed that the attack was racially-motivated – and wondering whether they were the ones who had brutally murdered my wife in her own kitchen. That was one of the reasons that it was such a relief to be able to go and stay with Bernie, whenever it got too much for me living in the house where Angie and I had been so happy together. It came as quite a relief when I sold the house, because it meant I never had to go back and walk down the road feeling suspicious of every white face that I passed in the street.

But I'm getting ahead of myself. I need to talk about Angie's funeral, which was surprisingly revelatory for me. Angie's parents were far too old and frail to make the journey from Jamaica to England, but the family wanted to be represented. I have to admit that I thought it was a mistake when they decided that her brother Joseph would come. Naturally, I didn't say anything but it seemed like a mad idea for a man with cerebral palsy that was severe enough to put him in a wheelchair to attempt to cross the Atlantic, even with the help of a couple of his nephews.

Of course, I was wrong. And I was also wrong to worry about his insistence that he wanted to speak during the funeral. I hadn't met him since that first time when Angie and I went over there for our honeymoon, so I was surprised how much his speech had come on. It was still sometimes a bit jerky and I could imagine people who didn't know him thinking that he might be a bit drunk, but it was completely understandable. You could have heard a pin drop during the service while he explained all about everything that Angie had done for him when he was a child and then afterwards when she came to England to learn more about the therapy that could help him to find his voice, and to earn the money to pay for it. I felt tremendously proud of her – and humbled to think that she had chosen to marry me instead of going back to the family that meant so much to her.

Then, after Joseph had given his testimony, the whole congregation seemed to explode as people all wanted to tell their own story about how Angie had helped them or how kind she had been when they had been on her ward in the hospital or what a good friend or colleague she was. Bernie told me afterwards that some of them were people that she knew would never normally agree to speak in public. Even Eddie, who always refused when he was asked to read the lesson in church, stood up and talked about what a wonderful mother Angie was. I wish I could remember some of the things that people said. Perhaps that would make you understand just how marvellous she really was.

I started to wonder if I ought to get up and say something myself, but I couldn't think of anything that would go even half way to doing Angie justice. So I just sat there letting it all wash over me.

Well, that's the *death* bit over with. *Judgement* was a bit longer coming. In fact, I'd rather given up on the idea that we would ever know who killed Angie, never mind bring them to justice. MacBride came to see me to explain that the investigation was being stepped down. The file was being left open, but they weren't going to continue actively working on it. I understood completely. I'd seen too many unsolved cases in my time to be surprised. In a way, it was a relief to know that there was no danger that I would suddenly be confronted with the killers or be required to re-live everything in court.

I was calculating without taking DCI Jonah Porter into account!

After his disabling injury, Jonah was looking for a case to tackle to prove that he was still up to the job and ought to be allowed to return to work. When he heard that Angie's killers still hadn't been found, he decided to have a go at solving the case himself. Only Jonah could believe in himself enough to think of taking on a hopeless case like that one – and only Jonah could be proved right by coming up with the answer! It makes you sick, doesn't it? I bet MacBride felt a bit stupid when he found out.

I won't go into all the details. The main thing is that we discovered that it wasn't a white on black racist attack. The killer was a black youth – tanked up with drink, by all accounts, despite it being early morning, and wanting to show off to his friends – who thought it was racial treachery for a black woman to marry a white police officer. Jonah managed to get the story out of one of the other lads in the gang and after that, it didn't take long to round them all up. I suppose that, being in a wheelchair, Jonah didn't appear as threatening as most police officers. And, although it pains me to say so, he does have quite a way with him when it comes to interviewing reluctant witnesses.

They all got custodial sentences, apart from Leroy, the youngster who spilled the beans. I was glad about that. Leroy hadn't actually taken part in the attack – he'd been outside keeping watch – and he'd been very young (only fourteen) and impressionable at the time, and quite over-awed by the older lads. By the time we caught up with him, he seemed to have turned over a new leaf and had a young family of his own to support, which would probably have all gone by the board if he'd been sent to jail.

Another reason that I was glad that the judge gave him a community sentence, is that, unlike the others, he actually had been a neighbour of ours. He was living with his Grandmother, Celeste, in a house just over the road from ours. I knew Celeste slightly, and I'd seen Leroy as well, but I had never spoken to him or his younger brother, who was also living with their gran. Angie knew them all; and of course, Leroy knew Angie and knew that she was married to a policeman. Apparently, he told the others about that, and that was what prompted them to pay a call on our house. According to Leroy, they were expecting there to be nobody at home and they only intended to trash the place, not kill anyone.

I felt sorry for Leroy – I still do. He was only showing off to his 'friends', not intending anything to come of it, never mind somebody getting knifed to death. I wish he'd come forward sooner, but it's understandable that he was afraid of what would happen to him if he did. And, to be fair, he probably would have been taken into care, away from his gran, and maybe spent time in a young offenders' institution. They aren't great at rehabilitation – or not in my experience anyway – and he wouldn't have met the girl who gave him something more positive to live for. I'm glad he's building a life for himself now.

Leroy's younger sister, Stella, has become one of Lucy's friends. Lucy doesn't usually get on very well with her own age group. I think she finds them rather shallow, and they find her intimidating. Stella has enough life experience to be able to identify with Lucy's priorities around caring for Jonah and working to become a forensic pathologist. She's decided that she wants to be a police officer. I'm glad about that; we need more black officers in the service. I almost wish I hadn't retired so that I could have her in my team!

So, now we come to the *Future Life* part of this chapter. Well, I'll admit that the first couple of years after Angie's death were pretty grim for me. Bernie made it a whole lot better simply by being there and by allowing me to stay with her whenever it got me down to be living in the house that Angie had made into our home. It was difficult to sit in the front room of an evening, the way we always used to, and not be expecting her to come in any moment to join me. And when I went to bed, it always seemed strange that she wasn't there beside me – although, in fact, I'd often slept alone when she was working nights. And if the wind rattled the front door, I always felt an urge to go out into the hall to see if it was her coming in.

Hannah was very solicitous for my welfare, for which I tried to be grateful. Fortunately, she was far enough away that I only got the full force of her ministrations during brief visits. I'm sure she was grieving herself and looking after *poor old dad* was her way of coming to terms with her loss, but I'm afraid I found it rather wearing. I'm glad that she had Laurence to lean on during that period. Knowing that he was there with her made it a lot easier for me.

Eddie was different altogether. Being a young man, he wasn't demonstrative in his grief, but I know he felt the loss of his mother very much. At the time, I probably didn't realise this as much as I ought to have done; but it became very obvious when I announced that I was marrying Bernie. At first, Eddie simply wouldn't speak to me. Every time I rang, he slammed the phone down on me. He made it very clear that he couldn't accept the idea that I could even consider re-marrying so soon after Angie's death.

But, I'm getting ahead of myself again. Eddie, very bravely, went back and finished his degree. Then, to my enormous surprise, he announced that he was going to Jamaica to find his roots. He'd made friends with the cousins who had come over with his Uncle Joseph for the funeral, and one of them had found him a job in the computer firm where he worked. I didn't quite know what to make of this. I could identify with wanting to get away from home, with all the associated memories of happier times; but I wished it didn't have to be quite so far away. I was glad that he was going to be living near Angie's family, and maybe contributing to their, always precarious, finances; but I worried that this was because he felt that he didn't fit in back in England among our mainly white friends. The bottom line, however, was a recognition that it was his life, not mine, and at least he had a job – which was the biggest anxiety for most parents of new graduates.

I mentioned before that Bernie had been Eddie's friend and mentor for a long time. It was because he got on so well with her that I was completely taken aback when he couldn't accept our getting married. Jonah has a theory that Eddie had a crush on Bernie and it was partly jealousy that set him against the idea; but I think it was simply that he couldn't understand how *anyone*, even Our Bernie could replace his mother. In that respect, of course, he was right. That's why I married Bernie, who was the only woman in the world who could be relied upon to understand that and not to mind.

Well, there were a few other reasons, I suppose. Lucy was one of them. I'd always been a father-figure to her, and this put it on a proper official footing. The other main reason was that Bernie was the one person who knew Angie nearly as well as I did. They'd been friends for almost the whole of our married life; so there wasn't much that Bernie didn't know about her. Most people avoid mentioning Angie in front of me. They're afraid it will upset me, which it possibly might, but not as much as knowing that they are deliberately air-brushing her out of the conversation. And, because I know that it will make people embarrassed, I don't talk about Angie much either. That's why it's good to have Bernie around. She doesn't mind listening to my reminiscences – even if it does all end in tears sometimes – and she isn't afraid to bring up the subject herself. Best of all, I know that she sometimes really wants to talk about her best friend as much as I do.

6 FINAL WORDS

That about wraps things up. Looking back, I seem to have drifted away from the subject rather a lot. It's been hard to sum up Angie's life without talking a lot about other people. That's because she was so involved in other people's lives and gave so much to them. It's probably also because it's easier for me to talk about those things than about Angie herself, and especially about our relationship, which is very personal to me. I just hope that you will have got an idea of the wonderful person that she was. If, when you finish reading, you wish that you could meet her yourself, then I'll be satisfied that I've done what I set out to do.

Peter

THANK YOU

Thank you for taking the time to read MY LIFE OF CRIME. If you enjoyed it, please consider telling your friends or posting a short review. Word of mouth is an author's best friend and much appreciated. Thank you,

Judy.

ACKNOWLEDGEMENTS

I would like to thank the authors of a wide range of internet resources, which have been invaluable for researching the background to this book. These include (among others):

- Wikipedia (https://en.wikipedia.org/)
- Google Maps (https://www.google.co.uk/maps)
- GENUKI (http://www.ukbmd.org.uk/genuki/reg/)
- The National Meteorological Archive (http://www.metoffice.gov.uk/learning/library/archiv e-hidden-treasures)
- The Oxford Mail (http://www.oxfordmail.co.uk)
- Action for Children (https://www.actionforchildren.org.uk/)
- Oxford University Hospitals NHS Foundation Trust (http://www.ouh.nhs.uk/hospitals/jr/history.aspx)

Witness Evidence was inspired by the insights I gained through taking the FutureLearn course Forensic Psychology: Witness Investigation, delivered by the Open University. This free online course may be found here:
https://www.futurelearn.com/courses/forensic-psychology

MORE ABOUT PETER AND HIS FRIENDS

Peter and his wife Bernie feature in six more books.

- Awayday: a traditional detective story set among the dons of an Oxford college.
- Changing Scenes of Life: Jonah Porter's life story, told through the medium of his favourite hymns.
- Despise not your Mother: the story of Bernie's quest to learn about her dead husband's past.
- Two Little Dickie Birds: a murder mystery for DI Peter Johns and his Sergeant, Paul Godwin.
- Murder of a Martian: a double murder for Peter and Jonah to solve.
- Death on the Algarve: Peter and Jonah investigate an unexpected death while they are on holiday with Bernie and Lucy.

Read more about Bernie Fazakerley and her friends and family at https://sites.google.com/site/llanwrdafamily/

Visit the Bernie Fazakerley Publications Facebook page here:
   https://www.facebook.com/Bernie.Fazakerley.Publications.

Follow Bernie on Twitter: https://twitter.com/BernieFaz

ABOUT THE AUTHOR

Like her main character, Bernie Fazakerley, Judy Ford is an Oxford graduate and a mathematician. Unlike Bernie, Judy grew up in a middle-class family in the South London stockbroker belt. After moving to the North West and working in Liverpool, Judy fell in love with the Scouse people and created Bernie to reflect their unique qualities.

As a Methodist Local Preacher, Judy often tells her congregation, "I see my role as asking the questions and leaving you to think out your own answers." She carries this philosophy forward into her writing and she hopes that readers will find themselves challenged to think as well as being entertained.

COMING SOON: MYSTERY OVER THE MERSEY

Bernie, Peter and Lucy make a trip back to Liverpool to meet Bernie's relatives and see her old stamping grounds. They get more than they bargained for when Bernie discovers a corpse on the deck of a Mersey Ferry and rumours abound on social media that she could be responsible.

This new Bernie Fazakerley mystery will be published in 2017. To give you a flavour of things to come, here are the opening pages.

MYSTERY OVER THE MERSEY

A Bernie Fazakerley Mystery

by

Judy Ford

1 SHALL WE GATHER AT THE RIVER?

'Morning father! What can I do for you?' said the woman in the booking office at the Pier Head ferry terminal cheerily.

'Just a boarding card, please,' the young priest replied, holding up his *Trio* season ticket, which confirmed that he was entitled to unlimited travel on buses, trains and ferries throughout Merseyside.

'Here you are, love!' She printed the boarding pass and handed it across the counter. 'Don't forget you have to break your journey on the other side.'

The priest nodded rather absently, picked up his ticket and walked away. Behind him in the queue, Bernie Fazakerley moved up to the counter to claim boarding cards for herself, her husband Peter and her daughter, Lucy. Then she led the way out of the booking hall to where passengers awaiting the next crossing were standing by the gates to the landing stage, watching for the ferry to arrive.

It was more than three decades since Bernie had visited her home town. That had been to attend her father's funeral, after which there had seemed to be nothing there to make it worth her while going back. And she had not wanted to remind herself of the happy times of her childhood or give her numerous uncles, aunts and cousins an opportunity to commiserate with her over the death of her fiancé and her subsequent failure to find a replacement for him. They had all busily played happy families, sending her cards to announce births, marriages and, increasingly in recent years, deaths, while Bernie had lived alone for the best part of twenty years, devoting herself to her role of Tutorial Fellow at one of the lesser-known Oxford Colleges.

Marriage, when it did eventually come, had been to a police superintendent nearly nineteen years her senior, and Bernie had not felt it necessary or desirable to introduce him to the few remaining relatives with whom she still maintained sparse correspondence. She was beyond the age when she might have liked to show off her conquest and she was well aware that few would consider Richard Paige to be much of a catch. When he died a mere two years later, none of Bernie's Liverpool family attended the funeral, and only a few sent cards of condolence. Although she remained fiercely loyal to her native city, Bernie's life and friends were in Oxford – something that became increasingly clear after she gave birth to Richard's posthumous daughter, Lucy, and, at the age of forty-two, finally joined in the game of motherhood, which her Scouse cousins had been playing for so long without her.

Now Lucy was sixteen and was demanding to see the city that her mother always declared to be 'the best in the world'. Bernie, already feeling guilty at having neglected her family for so long, agreed to take her for a visit to see the sights and to meet her few remaining relatives. As always, her second husband, Peter, had come along for the ride – or more accurately, had come out of a mixture of affection for his stepdaughter, of whom he was extremely fond, and a sense of obligation to meet his in-laws, albeit rather distant ones.

The young priest looked rather out of place in his clerical collar and dark suit among the tourists in summer holiday garb eagerly anticipating their *River Explorer Cruise*. This was the rather grandiose description in the ferry company brochures of the round trip from Liverpool to two destinations on the Wirral side of the Mersey and back to the Pier Head. Bernie had shaken her head as she read the information and declared scornfully that this was not what it had been like in her day, when the ferries had been packed with workers travelling from homes on the Wirral to Liverpool, or conversely, travelling from Liverpool to the shipyards of Birkenhead. Then she had seen the price and had felt a mixture of pride in the ability of her fellow-Scousers to rip off the visitors and annoyance that she had become one of the victims of the racket. Finally, she had discovered that, for less than the cost of the so-called cruise, a *Saveaway* ticket could be purchased that allowed unlimited travel on rail, bus and ferry services for a day. That was more like it! And they could take the train to West Kirby or Port Sunlight – two fondly-remembered day-trip destinations from her childhood – for nothing.

The gate opened and they streamed down the slope towards the floating landing stage. The priest stumbled over the metal plate that covered the join between the ramp and the shore, allowing the landing stage to rise and fall with the tide. He seemed to be preoccupied and not watching his feet. He righted himself and walked briskly down to join the passengers queuing below. Bernie thought that he looked very young – quite unlike the ageing priests that she remembered from her childhood, with lined faces and grizzled grey hair; but perhaps that was just a sign of her own age, she mused, like what they said about how you knew you were getting old when the policemen started looking young. Lucy also watched the incident, noting subconsciously that, although the ferry brochure had boasted full accessibility, wheelchair users would need to take care during the process of boarding.

MV Snowdrop approached the landing stage and Bernie was afforded yet another opportunity to declare *it wasn't like this in my young day*! Not only had the ferry been re-named, but it had also been re-painted in a garish colour scheme as a *Dazzle Ship* – part of the World War I commemorations.

'It says here,' Lucy said, reading from her smartphone, 'that ships were painted like this in the war to make it more difficult for them to be targeted by German aeroplanes and U-boats.'

'Hmm!' her stepfather murmured, staring at the brightly patterned hull with a sceptical expression on his face. 'I understand the theory. It's like zebras having stripes to confuse the lions by breaking up their outlines;

but I can't help feeling that if I was manning the periscope on a U-boat I'd have no difficulty spotting all that red and yellow.'

'My gran used to tell us about the Mersey ferries going off to fight in the First World War,' Bernie told them. 'Not this one – they were steam ships in those days. And a couple of Dad's brothers went down in ships that were torpedoed in the Second World War. They were in the merchant navy bringing supplies from across the Atlantic.'

The ferry docked and passengers started to disembark. Then, shortly afterwards, the queue began to move and soon Bernie, Lucy and Peter were walking up the ramp on to the lower deck.

'Where shall we go?' Lucy asked

'There'll be a better view from upstairs,' Bernie told her, 'and I think you'll see more of the shore from the starboard side'.

So they climbed up to the stern deck and looked around for somewhere to sit. It was crowded and they could not see three seats together.

'Let's try the bow end,' Bernie suggested, leading the way forward, past the covered seating to what Peter, who was rather ostentatiously demonstrating that he had no pretentions to nautical knowledge, would insist on calling *the pointy end* of the boat. As they passed the door from the forward stairs, Bernie collided with the priest from the booking hall who was stepping out on to the deck, his head bowed.

'Sorry father,' Bernie apologised.

'No, no,' he murmured absently. 'My fault. I wasn't looking where I was going.'

Bernie stepped back and allowed him to go ahead of them. He took up a standing position at the front of the boat, leaning against the rail. Bernie watched as he reached into his pocket and took out a string of beads, which he raised to his mouth and kissed. He must be planning to spend the crossing praying the rosary. Bernie wondered briefly whether this was a regular discipline – a way of making use of time that would otherwise be wasted during a routine journey that he made, perhaps every week – or if it symbolised a particular need for prayer at this time. The young man had seemed distracted right from when she had first stood behind him in the queue at the booking office. Bernie strongly suspected that there was something very particular on his mind and she felt curious to know with what intention he was offering his prayers.

They sat down on a bench seat facing the rail on the starboard (or as Peter put it, the right-hand) side of the vessel. An automated voice welcomed them aboard and went through a list of safety instructions. The sound of the diesel engines increased and they were off.

As they travelled downstream past the famous Liverpool waterfront, Bernie had to compete with the public address system in pointing out landmarks to Lucy and Peter. She also pointed out the folly of the ferry company in choosing a voice that could have come from anywhere to provide their commentary. 'If they're trying to give tourists a flavour of Liverpool, they could at least have got a Scouser to record it!'

'Maybe they thought it was more important to make it intelligible to everyone,' Peter suggested. 'Like the way they provided English commentaries at tourist attractions when we were in Portugal. It's all very well for us, because we've brought along our own interpreter, but your average Japanese tourist wouldn't have a clue what they were saying if it was in the local dialect.'

The boat turned, giving them a view of the estuary, and the disembodied voice invited them to look to see New Brighton and the lighthouse beyond. It went on to promote the Floral Pavilion theatre, which it claimed had recently enjoyed a revival of its fortunes.

'We used to go for days out in New Brighton,' Bernie told Lucy. 'There used to be a ferry from the Pier Head that went there, but they stopped them when I was about twelve. I think they finally realised that New Brighton was not destined to become a major seaside resort!'

It was not long before they were drawing up alongside the landing stage at the Seacombe ferry terminal. Passengers walked past them on their way to disembark.

'Do we get off here?' Lucy asked.

'No. We'll stay on to Woodside,' her mother told her. 'I want to show you the street where my posh Aunty Margaret lived. She thought she was a cut above the rest of the family because she married an insurance broker and went to live across the water. They had a house near Birkenhead Park. It may even still be there.'

Lucy disappeared round to the other side of the boat and leant on the rail, looking down at the landing stage, as passengers disembarked and a new group came aboard. Most of them headed for the larger stern deck, leaving only a handful of passengers in the bow area. Bernie glanced forward to see if Lucy was coming back, and noticed that the priest was still there, leaning against the rail, apparently engrossed in his prayers.

The ferry moved off again, turning round so that it was travelling upstream with the Wirral shore to their right. Bernie went to join Lucy on the port side of the boat, in order to show her the view of Liverpool from this side of the river. The Priest did not look up as she passed him.

After only a few minutes, it was time to make their way down to the lower deck ready to disembark. Lucy and Bernie walked back again to join Peter, who had remained in his seat overlooking the starboard side of the boat.

'I'm sorry to disturb you, father,' Bernie said to the priest as they passed, 'But we're nearly at Woodside. You have to get off here.'

He did not reply. Bernie touched him gently on the shoulder to attract his attention. Immediately she knew that there was something wrong. He remained completely unmoving – unnaturally so. She shook his shoulder, gently at first and then more strongly. He twisted round and slipped to the floor. For a moment Bernie and Lucy stood there staring down at him. He lay in his back staring up with lifeless eyes, his right hand still clutching a rosary of brown wooden beads.

They knelt down to examine him. Bernie undid the buttons of his jacket with the idea of helping him to breathe. As she did so, she felt a stickiness on the black shirt beneath. She looked at her fingers and saw that they were smeared with blood. There was a small hole in the shirt, which Bernie tore wider, trying to find the wound. Lucy, realising what she was doing reached over to help. They both looked at the pale flesh beneath the clerical shirt and then looked at each other in stunned disbelief.

'Peter!' Bernie called out sharply. 'He's been stabbed – in the chest.'

Peter ran over, looked down briefly and then turned to go.

'Stay here,' he ordered. 'See nobody moves anything. I've got to make sure no-one gets off the boat.'

2 YE WHO HAVE WAITED LONG

'Please return to your seats,' came the announcement over the public address system. 'There has been a serious incident on board and we are awaiting the arrival of the police. Until then, no one is permitted to disembark. Mersey Ferries apologises for the inconvenience that this may cause.'

Bernie relinquished the body to two members of the crew, who stood guard over it, fending off passengers who crowded round wanting to know what was going on. After a few minutes of jostling, one of them tied ropes across the deck to keep everyone except Lucy, Bernie and the two guards away from the bow area.

Meanwhile, on the lower deck, Peter watched as the gangway was secured again in an upright position to prevent anyone leaving the vessel. He was glad that he had been able to intervene in time and that the deck hands in charge of docking the ship and supervising the disembarkation had accepted his authority as an ex-policeman and immediately suspended their operation. They summoned the first officer, who hurried upstairs to see the casualty for himself. Having confirmed that the young man was dead, he relayed the news to the captain who summoned the police and ordered everyone to stay on board until they came. Now the first officer and one of the deck hands were standing awkwardly by the body, to which their eyes kept being drawn involuntarily, and giving non-committal answers to questions from passengers who wanted to know when they would be allowed to leave the boat.

Bernie and Lucy sat down on one of the wooden seats on the bow deck, trying to keep out of the way and look inconspicuous.

'Are you alright?' asked the first officer, looking anxiously towards Bernie.

She followed his eyes downwards and saw for the first

time that her own shirt was stained with blood. It must have been transferred as the body slid down past her when she disturbed it.

'Yes,' she assured him. 'This isn't my blood – it must have come off him when I tried to attract his attention. I didn't realise he was dead,' she went on, trying to explain what she had been doing. 'I thought he just hadn't noticed we'd got to Woodside, and I was afraid he was going to forget to get off. So I put my hand on his shoulder and then he fell over.'

'It must have been a bit of a shock for you,' the first officer observed. 'Would you like me to get you a drink to steady your nerves?'

'No thanks. I'm fine.'

'This isn't the first time we've seen a dead body,' Lucy informed him. She had been disappointed at not being allowed to examine the wound more closely and wanted to make it clear that there was no need to shield her or her mother from the grim reality of violent death. 'Mam is personal assistant to a DCI and she sees murder victims all the time. And I'm going to be a forensic pathologist,' she added, 'so this is really good experience for me.'

'Are you now?' the first officer said, smiling indulgently.

'You'd better believe her,' Bernie said firmly. 'She's got it all planned out. And she's deadly serious when she talks about getting experience. She's already managed to persuade a friend of ours to let her sit in on a post mortem. So my advice is – don't mess with our Lucy, if you know what's good for you!'

'I'd better check if the police are on their way.' The first officer excused himself and left them.

They sat for a few minutes in silence. Then Lucy turned to her mother with a puzzled frown on her face.

'How come nobody noticed him being killed?' she wondered. 'I mean, there were people about – us for a start – and yet we didn't see or hear anything.'

'I suppose we weren't watching,' Bernie answered. 'And there weren't that many other people out here after we left Seacombe.'

'But you'd have thought he'd have shouted out,' Lucy persisted. 'I mean, it must have hurt, mustn't it? But I don't remember hearing a thing.'

'I don't know. Maybe you don't feel much if the knife goes straight into your heart. Or maybe it killed him so quickly he didn't have time to call out.'

'Could he have done it himself do you think?'

'I'd be surprised,' Bernie shook her head. 'For starters, he's a Roman Catholic priest. He must have had it drummed into him that suicide is a mortal sin. And I doubt if it's possible to kill yourself by stabbing yourself through the heart. It must take some force to do it. I don't know, but I think your reflexes would probably stop you. And whoever did it pulled the knife out again afterwards. Why would you bother if you were killing yourself? But if you're a murderer, you want to get rid of the murder weapon. And,' she continued, pointing towards the priest's right hand, which still clutched the rosary, 'he couldn't have held a knife in his right hand because it was already full.'

'What will the police do next?' Lucy wanted to know. 'I suppose they'll want to interview us?'

'They're bound to,' her mother agreed. 'But the first thing they'll want to do is to secure the crime scene, to make sure that no evidence is lost. Those ropes are a start, but the whole ship will have to be checked over by a forensics team. Whoever did it is likely to have blood on them somewhere, so they may want to check everyone's clothing. It's all going to take a long time, I'm afraid. Somehow I fancy we may not be going to get to see Aunty Margaret's house today, after all.'

'Never mind. This is much more exciting,' Lucy said, getting up and going over to look at the body more closely. She stood over it, staring down. 'I think you're right about it not being possible for him to have stabbed himself. If he had done, the hand that he'd held the knife in – which would have had to be his left hand – would be covered with blood. I mean – look at how much you've got on you, just touching him. His clothes are soaking in it.'

'Mmm. That's what makes me think the knife must have gone straight into his heart – or at least a major artery. Either the killer was dead lucky or he knew exactly what he was doing.'

'I don't suppose they'd let me sit in on the PM?' Lucy suggested, knowing already that the answer would be negative but determined not to allow the opportunity to pass without any attempt at taking advantage of it.

'No. I'm sure they wouldn't. And it's no good asking me or Peter to lobby on your behalf. It was all very well with Mike Carson, who knows us, but here we're just a couple of civilians who have no business getting involved. Besides, we are both witnesses, which means that it would be improper to allow you access to any additional evidence in case it biased your own testimony. In fact,' Bernie added, remembering an aspect of police procedure that she had forgotten in the excitement, 'we shouldn't really be discussing what we saw in case we influence each other's memories.'

Bernie's long association with the police, first through marriage and, during the two years since her retirement from academia, as the personal assistant to DCI Jonah Porter, meant that she had accumulated a large amount of knowledge about good practice in criminal investigation. She ran through in her mind the steps that the team from Thames Valley Police would have taken in these circumstances.

'I bet all the other passengers are discussing what they saw,' Lucy said combatively. 'So I don't see why we shouldn't'

'It's all a matter of making sure that our evidence is independent,' Bernie explained. 'According to the psychologists, witnesses naturally like to agree with one another, so what you say you saw might influence what I remember seeing. We don't like to feel that what we are saying is inconsistent with what other people tell us they saw. And then, precisely because our evidence is consistent, juries tend to believe that what we think we saw was what actually happened. Ideally, witness would all be kept in complete isolation until after they've given their statements to the police.'

'That must make everything take an awfully long time,' Lucy observed. 'I thought they'd interview the three of us all together.'

'They shouldn't,' Bernie said firmly. 'However, in your case they're in a bit of a bind, because there's also a rule that says that you can't interview minors without an appropriate adult present – which would normally mean me or Peter. You have to have someone there to look after your interests and see that they don't bully you.'

'Anyway, we'll have plenty to talk about with Cousin Joey and the rest of them tomorrow,' Lucy said, obediently seeking a topic of conversation that could not be construed as prejudicial to the enquiry. 'I bet they've never been witnesses to a murder.'

'No, I don't suppose they have – although the way some people talk, you'd think it was the sort of thing that happened every day in their part of Liverpool – and I'm not that overjoyed that we are, either,' Bernie said sharply. 'Before you get too excited about the whole business, please try to remember that somebody has actually died here.'

'Sorry, Mam,' Lucy tried to feel remorse. 'But we didn't know him and you have to admit it's interesting to try to think how someone managed to do it under our noses like that – and why they'd want to, as well. What harm could a priest have done to anyone?'

'And that's another thing,' her mother answered, refusing to be drawn in to speculation. 'Two of Joey's uncles and one of his brothers are priests, so it's entirely possible that they could have known this one. So be very careful what you say to the family tomorrow.'

'Who exactly is it we're meeting?' Lucy forced herself to move the conversation on to safer ground. 'I get so confused trying to work out who everyone is.'

'Joey is my cousin. His dad was my dad's brother, so he's another Fazakerley. He and his wife, Ruth, have invited us over. Joey's mum is a widow and getting on a bit, so she lives with them and I expect we'll see her too. Her name is Rose. Then Joey and Ruth have three kids: James, Chloë and Dominic. They're all still living at home as well.'

'How old are they?'

'I can't remember exactly. Dominic was just a baby when I married your dad. I remember because that was Joey's excuse for not coming to the wedding. So I suppose he must have been born in ninety-six or maybe early in ninety-seven. He's the youngest, by quite a few years.'

'So they're all a lot older than me.'

'It depends what you mean by *a lot*, but yes, they're all in their twenties. You have to remember that my dad was the youngest in his family and then I left it rather late to have you, so the surprising thing really is that there isn't a bigger age gap.'

'So aren't there any *young* relations for me to meet?'

'Not that I know of. At least … there must be lots, but they've probably moved away. The only people I've kept up with are Joey and Aunty Dot. She's one of my dad's sisters. She never married, so she helped us out when my mam was diagnosed with motor neurone disease. She was a bit like a second mother to me. We're going to see her tomorrow as well. She's in a care home in Wavertree. Joey's going to take us over there tomorrow afternoon.'

'Your attention please,' the captain's voice sounded over the public address system again. 'The police have now arrived and arrangements are being made for you to disembark. Please remain in your seats for further announcements. Once more, I would like to apologise for the delay to your journey and the inconvenience that it will cause.'

'I bet he's glad it will be the police's job to break it to them all that getting off the ship is only the start of things,' Bernie muttered. 'I imagine there's a lot going on clearing the ferry terminal and finding somewhere to accommodate us all while we wait to be interviewed and fingerprinted and stuff.'

'Jonah will be green with envy when he hears that we've got involved in a murder without him,' Lucy said, smiling at the thought of their friend from Thames Valley CID, whom they had left behind in Oxford. 'This is just the sort of thing he'd enjoy investigating.'

'Too right, he would,' her mother agreed, smiling at the mention of DCI Jonah Porter, who played a big part in both of their lives. 'Which means it's a good thing he stayed at home this time. If he was here, I'd have my work cut out preventing him from trying to take over – which would *not* be likely to endear us to the local CID.'

'I wonder how he's getting on at home with Nathan looking after him,' Lucy mused. 'He said he was going to give Nathan lots of jobs to do in the garden to keep him out of his hair, but I think Nathan was expecting to be fully occupied seeing to his personal care.'

'I expect they'll rub along OK. Nathan's a good lad. He's just never managed to stop being over-protective, that's all.'

A bullet in the neck, more than seven years previously, had left Jonah severely disabled. He had fought back and had demanded to be allowed to continue his police work. This was made possible by dint of an array of technological devices and by having Bernie as his constant companion during working hours. After his wife's death, Bernie and her family had played an increasing role in his care, culminating in his moving in with them on a full-time basis. Nathan, his younger son, was very willing but found it hard to allow his father the same freedom to take risks as he enjoyed when Bernie was in charge. Lucy was quite correct in thinking that a week's annual leave in the care of his son, without the stimulation of his police work, would be a trying ordeal for him.

'I'll send him an email,' Lucy said, reaching in her pocket for her smartphone. 'It'll cheer him up to have a nice juicy murder to think about.'

'You'll do nothing of the sort,' Bernie retorted firmly. 'First off: you've no business telling anyone about this until the police say you can. And second, what business do you have suggesting that Jonah needs cheering up, just because he doesn't have you there to keep him amused? For all you know, he and Nathan are having a whale of a time!'

Lucy looked sceptical, but replaced her phone in her pocket.

'I bet none of the other passengers are maintaining radio silence,' she muttered. 'They'll all be on to their friends and relations saying,' – and here she switched to an exaggerated version of her mother's Liverpool accent –, 'Get this, Our Kid. I've got a right cob on with this malarkey. It's cracking the flags down here and we've got to stay on this ferry boat while the filth faff about asking questions.'

'Not so much of the cheek, our Lucy!' Bernie pretended to be offended. 'Never mock a Scouser – we have long memories. Seriously, though, I'm glad that we're the only people who actually saw anything. It'd be awful if his,' – here she looked down at the dead priest lying at their feet –, 'family got to hear rumours before he's been officially identified.'